Weatherwise

Practical Weather Lore for Sailors and Outdoor People

Paul John Goldsack

DAVID & CHARLES

Newton Abbot   London   North Pomfret (Vt)

British Library Cataloguing in Publication Data

Goldsack, Paul John
    Weatherwise: practical weather lore for sailors
    and outdoor people.
    1. Folklore—Great Britain   2. Weather lore—
    Great Britain
    I. Title
    398'.363'0941   GR635

ISBN 0–7153–8788–X

© Paul John Goldsack 1986

Photoset in Baskerville by
Northern Phototypesetting Co Bolton
and printed in Great Britain
by Redwood Burn Limited Trowbridge Wilts
for David & Charles Publishers plc
Brunel House Newton Abbot Devon

Published in the United States of America
by David & Charles Inc
North Pomfret Vermont 05053 USA

CONTENTS

Author Goldsack sniffing the wind: 'shall we, shan't we put to sea today . . .'

Chapter One

FOR STARTERS

When I was no more than a minnow I used to haunt the shed of a bawleyman who went seeking shrimps out of the Kentish river. 'It ain't the Medway, boy', he admonished with a voice that rumbled like the surging grate of a capstan chain; 'it's the Kentish river to us Kentishmen and Men-o-Kent, remember that.' And so I have. It has been the Kentish river ever since, just as the Thames has always been the 'London river' to east-coast sailormen.

In those far off days it is unlikely that I knew what an east-coast man was, for I was little more than knee-high to a trouser stain and just as short on knowledge. I think I must have been about twelve when I found out, after an uncle who was renowned within the family for grit and grump reluctantly gave me my first sail beyond the Kentish estuary to the rivers Blackwater, Colne and Crouch. By the end of that week's lazy cruise I had become a life-long, Stockholm-tar-dyed, mud-wallowing sailor of the rivers and creeks of south-east England and East Anglia. That's what an east-coast sailor is.

Since those days of my first childhood, and far into my second, I have sailed beyond those tiny water-splinters in England's coastline. I have swooped the Atlantic rollers, sought out the north-east trade winds, reefed deep-keelers down Channel, and nosed into sun-bathed Mediterranean harbours. They have been good times. But best of all I have loved the days and nights when I coasted from the Alde to Greenwich in spritsail barges or shared the solitude of an isolated mud-creek with the eerie shrieks of unseen wildfowl. I was in honourable company, sailing with the spirits of my forefathers, sharing the secret sumps and swatches which before me have carried the shoal-draft little ships of Arthur Ransome and Francis Cooke and Maurice Griffiths – all fine writers, all east-coast men. Like them, I too am proud to have cheated the estuary tides.

I am told by those who cannot understand the affliction that we east-coasters become bores about our love for the saltings, the mud flats, and our endless panegyrics about the lost lands and the wild places of Essex, Kent and Suffolk. So I realise, only too well, that a good many leisure-time sailors never wish to seek, and so will never find, the magic of the creeks that meander like grey eels through stranded shoals of glistening mud whales. But their loss may indeed be a blessing, for it means that the

Fair-weather cumulus and a brown-sail Thames spritty 'that used to pound past on the evening tide . . .'

lonely creeks are left to just a fortunate few while others go in search of endless horizons and blue-deep waters where the steersman is not forever crying 'Lee-ho!' as his centreboarder noses yet again into the ooze banks of burnt-sienna gutways.

Like those who travel upon deep oceans, I too have taken passage from Ushant to the Scillies and beyond. But unlike most of them, I have never forsaken my first love and so returned, yet again and again, to the swatchways. In my heart of hearts I know exactly why I am reluctant to stay away – it is nothing more than an emotional search for those perfect, seemingly endless summers of youth. Sadly, though, the memories are now fading.

What happened to the brown-sailed work boats that once pounded past on the evening tide, and all the wooden lighters which used to bustle up-river like fussy ducklings behind tip-nosed mothers called *Tug It* and *Lug It* and *Pull It?* And all those boatyards which used to echo summer long to the ratter-pounding of caulking mallets. Where are they now? And why, oh why, is the big-ship smell of Stockholm tar no longer in the air? Silly questions – they have all blown away on the relentless winds of time; can it really be all to our good?

I suppose so, for the perfect wooden cruisers of my daydreams are in reality more ponderous, less slippy quick, than the sleek fibre-glass possessions of eighties man. No matter that many of them look like bathroom furniture, while my ancient timber beauties are far cosier, often more sea-kindly, and always much, much more likeable. I know, probably better than anyone, that the oil lamps which cast flickering, intriguing shadows across the cabin stink obnoxiously at times, but they never dim or die because someone has forgotten to charge the batteries. Like my wooden masts and wooden hulls, though, they are forever needing care and attention. Indeed, even I get brassed off at times when my lunatic passion for nostalgia results in the stench of paraffin over my hands or the reek of tar permeating everything, including my clothes; or when winter winds blow up the estuary and I am left to rub down my brightwork alone while the rest of the world shrouds its hulls in rot-proof plastic and slinks off for a beer.

Which, in a somewhat roundabout route, brings me at last to where I was heading. For it was during just one such period of solitude some twelve years ago that I fell to musing on the iniquities of our weather forecasts; you tend to muse a good deal as you grow older. It was, I remember clearly, a golden day in late summer when no more than a very gentle southerly breeze licked tiny wavelets around the boats idling at the trots. They should not have been idle that Saturday, for their owners were a more than normally enthusiastic band of sailors. Indeed, they would have been up and away many hours since had not the previous evening's broadcast predicted the coming of strong and wet north-easters.

Sailors should never pin their faith on Meteorological Office predictions, for they are far from infallible. About 85 per cent are reasonably accurate, 8 per cent contain errors of one sort or another, and the remaining 7 per cent are out and out 'howlers'. The figures are not mine but those of Sir John Mason, Director General of the Meteorological Office. In fact I would opine that he strayed more than a fraction or two on the optimistic side. In any case, he did not deny that there is room for improvement.

I carried out some research not long ago on the efficiency of our official forecasters and, in the manner of freelance journalists who like to believe that there will be a bob or two in everything they investigate, was not a little miffed to discover that Peter Dunn of *The Sunday Times* was onto the same story idea. He got into print quicker – bless the dexterity of his typing fingers! According to Dunn's eight months' log of the weather: 'the forecasts covering this little corner of south-east England have been monotonously on the wrong side throughout the year'. It should be pointed out that Dunn's 'little corner' was, in fact, an allotment in south London; only a fellow journalist would have expected the met boffins to accurately predict just when rain or sun was going to fall upon his 300 sq yd (250m²) scrap of land. Nevertheless, the premise holds good: met forecasts for the whole of the British Isles are often wrong; the predictions for local areas are rarely worth a light. These facts should register loud and clear with mariners.

Dunn's figures more or less verified my own: newspaper weather reports in *The Times* were right 82 times and wrong 150. Radio forecasts were wrong 107 times out of 504.

More recently still, the *New Scientist* reported observations conducted over three-monthly periods; the official forecasts turned out to be correct on 39 occasions, doubtful on 14 and completely, shambolically wrong on 40. It seems, in fact, that the ratio of Met Office rights compared with wrongs has grown worse, not better, over the last thirty years or so. In the 1950s, official statistics claimed that 24-hour forecasts were 90 per cent accurate, and in 1969 they were supposed to be between 70 and 80 per cent on the right side of wrong. Nowadays, it seems, there is no better than a fifty–fifty chance that the forecast for your local area will be anywhere spot on.

Whatever can have gone wrong? Well, the Met Office isn't saying. Could it be that the £6 million super Cyber computer installed at the Meteorological Office in Bracknell, Berkshire, during 1983 cannot cope? My self-confessed lunatic view of all things ultra-technical is reflected in an unbecoming smirk of glee following the discovery that a high-cost electronic idiot such as the Bracknell monster may be unable to handle the analytical calculations entrusted to it.

There is, so far as I can make out, little chance that our official forecasters are going to get any better for a long, long time. The problem is that British weather is not only a capricious business, but a very local one as well. And how the met men glory in that awful place:

> *Did you see*
> *The B.B.C. . . .?*
> *The whole of England has a drought,*
> *But 'Local' is of course left out;*
> *When the country's drenched in rain,*
> *How come 'Local's' never the same?*
> *Or sun is shining totally,*
> *Except in places 'Locally'?*
> *Blizzards, storm and squall,*
> *Thunder, icy roads . . . they're all,*
> *Occurring somewhere parochial;*
> *Where is this awful place called 'Local'?*

It all comes down to the fact that we must learn to interpret general weather patterns – which, by and large, the Met Office can provide – in the context of where we live or sail. What is the real likelihood, for instance, that a sloop running down Channel is certain to experience the same weather off North Foreland as a yacht bound up the coast of Suffolk? Yet that is the area covered by *The Times* weather forecast before me as I write. Or what are the chances that a boat sailing on the northernmost fringes of sea area Dogger is going to receive the same winds and visibility as a vessel in the south of that same area? Yet they both get the same shipping forecast via the BBC.

Coastal area forecasts serve us a little, but not much, better. After all, everyone must have experienced from time to time the sudden changes of wind and sea conditions which can occur only a mile or so up the coast. I clearly remember once beating up Channel a mile or so off Plymouth into a muddled jumble of waves and winds which I estimated as Force 5, gusting 6 to 7, while nearer the shoreline other vessels were dawdling about in a silk-calm sea and a sloppy wind. Daft, isn't it, that we had all been offered the same forecast?

There can be no doubt that, despite the Met Office's deserved reputation for often getting it wrong, far too many of us amateur sailors pin too much faith on official forecasts. 'Heard the latest weather bulletin?' 'Winds light, becoming moderate later, south-westerly', comes the faint reply from across the water. And so we up anchor and make for the sea, confident that all will be blithe and disregarding the fact that the light wind which was flicking the leaves of poplar trees as we left home is now, already, gusting Force 4 to 5, and that the latest available forecast is clearly already out of date.

Getting the timing right is frequently the bane of meteorologists. They may accurately predict a change in wind direction and strength; but when – like where – is the problem. Therefore, in order to make up for official forecasting deficiencies we must learn to turn a general forecast into a local one – updating and amending, if necessary, the latest available information from the Met Office according to the state of the sky, the barometer, the birds and the bees and so forth.

I am well aware that countless pages of the yachting press, and not a few specialist weather-forecasting books for the yachtsman, have been crammed full with learned articles designed to teach us to become our own weathermen. But, by and large, they are such heavy reading that I suspect they have often done little more than muddy already murky waters. Unless you are one of the fortunate few with a liking for obscure terminology and have the sort of mind which can be bothered with excessive windage on the general structure of world weather which has very little to do with predicting for local areas, met studies can prove dreary dull. Which is one reason why it is time we got back to the simpler side of forecasting and approached the whole business the way Grandfather did. Who knows, he may have got it right.

Well, not always, he didn't. Something like eight years ago I set out to study and test the old saws of the countryside and sea. Did they make sense and, more importantly, were they accurate omens of the weather on the way? There were few clues. Generally speaking, all earlier writers had treated weather lores as quaint but primarily nonsensical old-wives' tales. Interestingly, though, American scientists didn't – a US 'scientific jury' deliberated long and hard in 1949 before ruling that 87 out of 153 old-English weather proverbs were true for North America in terms of scientific principles.

But it was not 'scientific principles' that I was after. I wanted to find out if any of our ancient weather lores actually worked. So I started to dig out what ended up as a collection of 2,793 old weather sayings. A good many were clearly idiotic, so they were scrapped early on. A lot merely repeated each other, so they were whittled out. The remainder were put to the test. In the event, not a single long-range adage made the grade. For example,

St Swithin's Day, if thou dost rain,
For forty days it will remain;
St Swithin's Day, if thou be fair,
For forty days 'twill rain nae mair,

not only looked an unlikely candidate for the category of accurate sayings, but was proved so upon subsequent investigation. In 1924, for instance, London had more than thirteen hours of sunshine on 15 July, St Swithin's Day. Then rain fell amost continuously for a month or more and it turned out to be the wettest summer in nearly

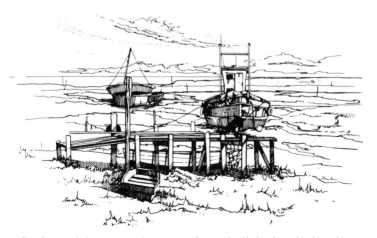

Gentle, steady breezes, a wisp or two of mares' tail clouds and only an hour to wait for the incoming tide

half a century. Given the fickle fancies of Britain's weather, how can any conditions be expected to remain constant for forty days? If, as very occasionally happens, the weather does settle into one pattern or another for so long, it is the exception rather than the rule.

There were a number of crushing disappointments. Many adages scored less than the 65 per cent accuracy factor arbitrarily chosen as the minimum necessary for inclusion among the reliables. So, out of the 2,793 I originally started out with, I eventually ended up with 231 which, after testing on a minimum of fifty separate occasions, proved reliable weather omens.

Most of these scored 80 per cent, indicating that they can be trusted eight times out of ten and therefore rate 'very good'. A few – those proving reliable seven times out of ten – are considered 'good'. Very many, though, scored a 90 per cent accuracy mark, and some can be counted on 100 per cent of the time; these are rated throughout the book as 'excellent'.

Finally, it became apparent fairly early in my

researches that weather lores should only form a single part of the armoury of forecasting. Clouds, sky signs, the barometer and, to some extent, the birds and the bees, all provide excellent clues to the local weather on the way; but they are best used in conjunction with official Met Office reports, whether as amendments or as updatings. Often the signs around us provide a clear indication that the general weather forecast from the Met Office is wrong. Often they enable us to fill in the precise local weather details which are omitted from area reports.

Weather saws alone, like the Met Office, are not infallible. Nor is the barometer. But together, the prediction sources at our disposal provide the maximum available information. They deserve to be used.

Chapter Two

SUN-UP, SUN-DOWN

We products of progress, descendants of yesteryear's sons of the soil, tend to look upon our yeoman forefathers as dumpling-cheeked, dim-witted old buffers with one hand to the plough and the other tugging the forelock beneath an empty, gormless pate. Don't you believe it. They cannot have been so daft, for they were a lot brighter than us when it came to predicting precisely when and where rain would fall. They, you see, knew how to read the sky.

The lores about clouds and sky colour bequeathed to us by past generations are among the most valuable of all weather signs, if only we have sense to use them. They are more reliable than most of the bewitching adages about birds and the beasts, just as knowing as messages in the wind, and just as apparent as the ups and downs of a barometer – once we learn to see again. And probably one of the very best signs of all is sky colour which provides, as it nearly always does, the first hints on the 'feel' of the day.

> *Red sky at night,*
> *Shepherd's delight;*
> *Red sky in morning,*
> *Shepherd's warning.*

Substitute the word 'sailor's' for 'shepherd's' if you prefer; the end result is still the same – one of the very few ancient weather lores which we still remember and even, more or less, trust. Grandmothers quote it, parents repeat it, toddlers learn to believe in it.

15

But does it make sense? Scientifically speaking, yes. The soft under-belly of cloud blushed pink by the sinking sun indicates clear sky and dry air to the west, and as most of Britain's weather either creeps or races in from westwards, 'this is typical of clearing weather following the passage of a cold front; as long as winds are from the west, as is usual, it is most unlikely for a further front to follow before the next day and bring bad weather', explain the meteorological pundits.

But does it make sense in practice, for scientific theories are notorious for turning topsy-turvy when pressed to the test? Do red skies at night signify a fine night followed by serene skies the following day? They should, for the very reason that man has been quoting the adage in one form or another since time immemorial. It even appears in the Old Testament and again in the New:

> *When it is evening, ye say It will be fair weather; for the sky is red. And in the morning, It will be foul weather today; for the sky is red and lowring.* (Matthew 16:2–3)

Despite its historical authenticity, though, my initial investigations uncovered the surprising fact that it is not to be invariably counted on. Tests conducted just after World War I by Spencer Russell over a six-year period indicated that fine weather followed upon the heels of a red sunset on only 111 occasions out of 161 – a disappointing 69 per cent which is no more than on the borderline of a 'good' accuracy tag. In fact, with profound apologies to Russell, my own tests suggest that the saying is far more dependable than that. I believe it is because he and I have interpreted the word 'red' in different ways.

A truly 'red' good-weather sunset sky is one that ranges from a virgin blush of pink to deeper, brighter, pastel hues of crimson plush; these are indeed shepherd's and sailor's delights with test results qualifying the adage for a reliability factor close on 100 per cent. A total of 97 fine nights and 77 fine tomorrows followed 102 observations of what I considered a 'proper' good-weather red sunset. But a lurid evening sky – one that is angry, livid red or orange – is one to be wary of; furl your sails and guard your anchor, put away your walking boots and stay at home, for 77 garish, over-vivid evening sunsets observed during tests were followed by 74 bad-weather nights and 61 grey, wet and gloomy days.

Always beware gaudy sky colours at any time of day. Light, delicate-coloured tints together with quilt-plump clouds as soft as candy floss, on the other hand, foretell dry and generally fine weather for at least the next twelve hours.

Only experience can teach us how to distinguish the colours which omen good weather from those which warn of deteriorating conditions or, quite often, absolutely nothing of significance at all. Great-great grandfather probably found it easy. For the ploughmen and seamen of the nineteenth century and before, the subtle shade differences between good and bad sky omens were, no doubt, just as obvious as seemingly invisible animal spoor still is for native trackers in the wild places of the world. The untrained eye cannot detect where passing hooves have crushed the grasses or scuffed the rocks, just as we nowadays-people are unable to properly see the colours in the sky or accurately distinguish and interpret different cloud formations. Our livelihoods no longer depend upon it, and so we have lost the habit of looking. Yet every single weather fact of past, present and future is logged somewhere in the sky – the remnants of what has gone before are mingled with the signs of what is here and now, jumbled with the odds and ends which indicate what is still to come.

It is because we have blindly sought to apply a few of the

well-remembered weather lores, which we do not properly understand, to the skies and other natural phenomena, which we do not properly see, that they have gained the reputation of being unreliable and then scornfully jettisoned as nothing more than foolish old wives' tales or retained because they are merely the quaintly expressed leavings of our forefathers. We, too, must learn to distinguish a watery-yellow sky which omens rain, from the yellow-sky flecks which presage nothing of any great significance; and the angry orange sunset which indicates the likelihood of deteriorating weather, from the gentle orange-red which promises a fine tomorrow.

The old lores can teach us what to be on the look out for and, once properly indentified, what weather is on the way. And, as the adage has it,

> *Best time to say,*
> *What weather's on the way,*
> *Is at the start and end of day.*

RED SUNRISE

> *Red sky in the morning,*
> *Is a sailor's sure warning.*

Reliability rating: excellent. Remember, though, that angry hues whether seen in the morning, at noon, or towards nightfall, are bad-weather omens, whereas light and peaceful colour tints predict finer weather. Given a lurid-red sunrise, always forecast the probability of wind and rain later in the day. There are six possible permutations all to do with a bright red sunrise and with wind behaviour at the time:

1 With a veering wind: short outbreaks of rain, temporary lull in the wind followed by clearer skies, showery outbreaks and wind squalls. Note, however, that

A brilliantly clear sunrise when all seems bright and clean portends a dull day about nine times out of ten

if the morning sky perceptibly lowers and becomes ever more gloomier, a major deterioration is very possible. Check wind lores (Chapters 11 and 12), clouds (Chapters 6, 7 and 8) and barometer (Chapter 14).

2 With backing wind: rain imminent (probably only a matter of minutes away), strengthening winds – probably Force 5–7, maybe even stronger.

3 With westerly wind: rain probable within ten to fifteen hours on average, sometimes much sooner dependent on

the amount of red in the sky – the angrier, the redder the sunrise, the closer the rain and wind are likely to be. Wind will increase and back accompanied by a fall in air pressure: barometer falling 1–2 millibars in three hours indicates probable future wind strengths of Force 4–6; barometer falling 3 millibars or more in three hours presages stronger, maybe gale force, winds.

4 With southerly wind: sky will become overcast within about four hours (maybe sooner), bringing continuous moderate rain and backing, increasing wind within about five hours on average.

5 With easterly wind: mainly cloudy, periods of rain and drizzle which could persist throughout the day. No significant increase in wind strength.

6 With northerly wind: rain showers, increasing at first but dying away around noon. Wind will probably be gusty, falling during the afternoon as cloud cover decreases.

In all the above circumstances it is important to note the following adage:

> *Probability of rain following a red sunrise depends on the character of the clouds and their height above the horizon.*

Reliability rating: very good, providing the weather watcher sticks to the provisos contained in the next quotation.

Most of the adages included in this book are, so far as one can tell, exceedingly old; their origins have been lost somewhere along the passage of time and are now only attributable to an anonymous ancestor. This one is an exception, being neither particularly old, nor anonymous; for it was originated in the nineteenth century by C. L. Prince. He wrote:

If at sunrise small reddish-looking clouds are seen low on the horizon, it must not always be considered to indicate rain. The probability of rain under these circumstances will depend on the character of the clouds and their height above the horizon. It has frequently been observed that if they extend ten degrees, rain will follow before sunset; if twenty or thirty degrees, rain will follow before two or three pm; but if still higher and nearer the zenith, rain will fall within three hours.

Reliability rating: accurate 181 times out of 219 – 83 per cent accuracy. There is really nothing else to add; Prince has said it all. Note, however, the wind saying included under the sub-heading High Dawn/Low Dawn below, and the following two red-sunrise sayings.

A red sky in the morning when the clouds overhead are moving towards the east, means rain and a lowering sky is threatened.

Reliability rating: very good, forecasts an eight out of ten chance of a backing wind accompanied by a falling barometer, rain within at least ten to fifteen hours and a wind which is likely to become Force 5–8 (probably south-westerly or south-easterly) within six to twelve hours. These are the classic signs of an approaching depression with grizzly-grey skies, high winds and rain (see also Chapters 13 and 14).

An additional hint: headsail and mainsheet ropes, especially if they are of cotton, feel distinctly clammy in the early morning and at night when a warm front is heading your way, while the day assumes a strange and translucent greyness; watch the barometer closely.

When the sun at rising assumes a reddish colour and shortly afterwards numerous small clouds collect, rain is expected within a few hours.

21

Reliability rating: very good. A gathering of clouds after a red sunrise forewarns that there is an eight times out of ten chance of the sky gradually becoming totally overcast. If it does, the red elements in the early morning sky denote that the clouds almost certainly carry rain and, possibly, an increasing wind.

HIGH DAWN/LOW DAWN

A 'high dawn' is when the first gleamings of sunlight appear over a bank of high cloud. A 'low dawn' is when sunrise breaks over the horizon into a cloudless, or near cloudless, eastern sky.

> *A high dawn indicates wind,*
> *a low dawn promises fair weather.*

Reliability rating: definitely something of a curate's egg deserving a mixed bag of ratings ranging from very good to good to plain indifferent. On average, the chances of a high dawn indicating wind – implying a more than normal increase in daytime strength – are no better than fifty-fifty. Given a high dawn *with* a red sunrise, the probability factor of rain occurring within three hours, and higher winds shortly after, increases to better than eight out of ten.

The probability of a low dawn promising fair and dry weather for the next twelve hours or so is not so good – no better than fifty-fifty.

GREY SUNRISE

> *A grey sky to the east at first light presages fine weather,*
> *but dark clouds towards the west indicate a strong*
> *possibility of rain.*

Reliability rating: excellent. During a grey sunrise even the grumpiest of skippers – and which of them is not – should be able to find a word or two of good cheer, for the likelihood of a fine, dry day is high. But keep the options open, do not flow with too much milk of human kindness if there is a forbidding-looking cloud or two looming up from westward.

Given a nicely packaged, straightforward grey dawn, there is a nine out of ten chance that the day will remain at least dry, if not exactly fine, for the next twelve hours or so. Given a grey dawn with dark clouds approaching from the west, skippers may retain their normal gloomy outlook until they get a chance of judging the quality of future cloud formations; in fact, during observation tests, when a grey sunrise was accompanied by gloomy clouds in the west rain occurred on six occasions out of ten. It all depended on the type of cloud which was approaching (see Chapters 6–8).

SUNSHINE SUNRISE

Too bright a morning breeds a louring [lowering] day.

Reliability rating: excellent – the antithesis, more or less, of the preceding 'grey sunrise' adage.

A brilliantly clear sunrise with excellent visibility, when all around appears bright and clean, portends a dull, overcast day just under nine times out of ten.

Don't be too despondent, though, for it won't necessarily rain. Only on about a fifty-fifty basis did rain – either heavily and consistently, or in showery fits and starts – fall during the twelve hours following clear, bright dawn observations.

CLOUDY SUNRISE

If at sunrise the clouds are driven away, then prophesy the coming of fine weather.

Reliability rating: very good. Whenever overhead clouds start to break up with the first signs of the morning light –

usually, although not always, along with a grey dawn – there is a better than 80 per cent chance that the next six hours, at least, will see sunny intervals and moderate to fresh winds. But keep checking sky-sign weather lores during the day for clues on whether it will be only a temporary improvement or a longer-lasting one.

RAIN AT SUNRISE

If rain begins at early morning light,
T'will end ere day at noon is bright.

Reliability rating: very good for this is one of the many old lores which imply that rain over British waters seldom lasts more than four to six hours; it doesn't, 83 per cent of the time. But the adage is not to be counted on outside the months May to September.

SUNRISE WINDS

The smaller and lighter winds of sunrise strengthen in
the morning and fall away towards sunset.

Reliability rating: excellent. One of the unwritten laws of British weather is that winds rise at dawn and subside at dusk. There are, however, occasions when it does not apply – when the morning is heavily overcast, for instance, or when the temperatures are judged abnormal for the time of year.

SEA AT SUNRISE

If at dawn the sea is darker than the sky, the day will be
a settled one.

Reliability rating: excellent. I shall not attempt to provide a plausible explanation for this adage, nor am I sure there actually is one. Suffice to say that in practice it turned out to be accurate ten times out of ten; invariably whenever the sea appeared darker than the sky at first light (usually on one of those mornings when there was a light cast of cloud right across the sky) the day slowly turned to a fine one.

If the sea appeared noticeably lighter than the sky, the weather turned out to be decidedly poor, unsettled, and the time for wise sailors to seek out other omens.

BLUE SKY AT DAWN

If the sky just after dawn is dark and steely blue, anticipate wind. If light blue, the day will be fine with mainly light to gentle winds.

Reliability rating: excellent. Dark-blue dawn skies, as hard as enamel, were followed by fresh to strong winds on 117 occasions out of 124. The difficulty arises, sometimes, when there is no more than a very thin dividing line between what may be a dark, steel-blue sky and one that is a softer, lighter blue. If there is a doubt in your mind then err on the safe side and expect the arrival, later in the day, of a freshening wind; it is unlikely to be over-strong.

My investigations lead me to believe, although I am still not absolutely sure, that the darker the blue then the fresher the approaching wind. Certainly, a light-blue sky promises nothing more than light to moderate breezes.

SUN SHAPE AT SUNRISE

If the sun appears concave at its rising, the day will be windy or showery; windy if the sun be only slightly concave, and showery if the concavity is deep.

Reliability rating: unknown. Sir Francis Bacon, who was unable to keep his nose out of anything remotely scientific, died in 1626 after catching a chill while stuffing snow up a chicken's carcass to see if it could be preserved. He dabbled, among all manner of things, in matters meteorological, penning, whenever the urge took him, the results of his observations. Most prove as daft as they seem. This one, though, offers fascinating possibilities and is included because my initial observations indicate that it might, just might, be true.

SUNRISE AND SUNSET

If the evening is red and the morning grey,
It is the sign of a bonnie day;
If the evening's grey and the morning red,
The lamb and ewe will go wet to bed.

Reliability rating: excellent, provided all the maybes and whereases outlined above on red and grey sunrises are taken into account along with all those on sunset sky signs which follow.

RED SUNSET

Red sky at night,
Is a sailor's delight.

This, perhaps the best known of all the weather lores, has already been discussed on pages 15–17. The great thing to remember is that red, if it is to be a reliable portend of a fine tomorrow, must not be over vivid or over angry and generally too much of a good thing. Too much, too intense, a red or too much orange, and the coming night is much more likely to be an unsettled one while tomorrow's weather is entirely undecided.

Gentle, soft colours foretell good weather. That should always be the overriding, decisive factor.

Narrow, horizontal red clouds after sunset in the west
indicate rain before thirty-six hours.

Reliability rating: very good. Test observations indicate that the weather deteriorated considerably within thirty-

26

six hours of observing 'narrow, horizontal red clouds' just after the sun disappeared into the sea. In actual fact, though, it turned to rain within the specified time limit on only 57 per cent of observations.

> *The red sun setting with distinct outlines with or without a red sky about it, is a sure sign of a fine day tomorrow.*

Reliability rating: very good, scoring eight out of ten during tests.

> *Red west at sunset with no thick banks of dark-grey or black clouds will be followed by a fine day.*

Reliability rating: good, scoring seven out of ten, for a fine tomorrow; excellent, scoring nine out of ten, for a fine night.

> *If the sun sets with a very red eastern sky expect rain; if red to the south-east expect rain.*

Reliability rating: good – 63 per cent accuracy. I have interpreted this saying as referring to the purple-pinkish glow which from time to time appears after sunset and is known, officially, as the 'last purple light'. The rating might have been better were I sure of identifying properly what the adage means by a 'very red' eastern sky.

> *A good crimson sky at sunset, with the wind going round with the sun, is an excellent sign.*

Reliability rating: excellent, for predicting fine, clear weather overnight and into the following day. The maxim is a useful belts-and-braces reminder that it is always useful to have a back-up lore tucked up your sleeve. A red

Red sky at night is, indeed, a 'sailor's delight' – providing you can spot a good 'un from a bad 'un

sunset and a veering wind are two reliable indicators of a fine-weather night and day on the way.

ORANGE SUNSET

Brassy-orange clouds in the west at sunset indicate wind and maybe storm.

Reliability rating: good. The rating would have been a lot better if the adage differentiated between hard, over-vivid and angry orange sunsets and the soft, gentle ones of chocolate-box paintings. In fact the harder, the denser, the orange, the greater the likelihood of higher winds (not necessarily storm-force, though) and rain. An orange tint, on the other hand, signifies dry, fairly settled weather.

YELLOW SUNSET

A bright yellow sky at sunset presages wind; a pale-yellow one, wet.

Reliability rating: excellent according to many textbooks, but barely worth a grudging 'good' according to my observations. Yellow skies at any time of day pose a problem for weather watchers. According to a number of meteorological experts, in fact, there is only a fifty-fifty chance of yellow skies preceding fine, wet and/or windy days.

The adage was destined for the wastepaper basket as unreliable, but I am bound to admit that observations indicate a certain amount of truth in it. Rain, or at least an unsettled night, followed behind 133 of the 246 recorded yellow sunsets; often enough to suggest that there must be some sort of yellow clue up there for those with eyes to see.

I see the colour all right. I am merely unable to detect the difference between a yellow sky which, so far as I can make out, foretells nothing at all of significance, from one that presages wind and/or rain. I shall keep persevering; I wish you would too.

WATERY SUNSET

If the sun goes pale to bed,
T'will rain tomorrow, so 'tis said.

Reliability rating: very good; I am on a sounder footing here, although not much. Some watery-looking suns (which is what the couplet is referring to) so obviously carry rain in their eyes that only a complete dunderhead would miss them. Some are nowhere as easy to spot.

As a general guide, I ignore any sun that looks only vaguely watery. When a sun appears virtually brimming over, with water vapour surrounding it, I apply this weather lore and obtain about an eight out of ten accuracy rating. In any case I take the couplet at its word and only forecast for rain by the following morning – in other words about eight to ten hours' time.

CLOUDS AT SUNSET

When the sun goes down into a bank of clouds, it indicates the approach of bad weather.

Reliability rating: good, but scoring no better than seven out of ten because the old saw fails to mention that the cloud bank should be dark and threatening. If this proviso is included, the adage is worth a much better, in fact very good, rating of 84 per cent accuracy.

In any case it is worth noting that after any day of clear, blue skies, the sun setting low behind a cloud bank often provides the first indication that adverse weather is approaching, though often as much as two or even three days away.

Also worth bearing in mind is the following old lore:

When cotton-wool clouds become heaped up during a strong wind at sunset, thunder may be expected during the night.

Reliability rating: very good, so long as you merely suspect the chance of thunderstorms. There was the definite possibility of thunder on 27 observations out of 34, although it actually occurred on only 9 of those occasions.

If the sun behind a bank does set,
Westerly winds you'll sure to get.

Reliability rating: good, with a 67 per cent chance of proving accurate.

Chapter Three

TRUE OR FALSE

Fancy your chances as a weather prophet? Care to test your skills? If so, decide if the following old-time weather sayings are true or false.

1 *March comes in like a lion, and goes out like a lamb.*
2 *Rain before seven, fine by eleven.*
3 *A rainbow in the morning, sailor take warning; A rainbow at night, sailor's delight.*
4 *The louder the frog, the more the rain.*
5 *Mackerel sky, mackerel sky,*
   Never long wet and never long dry.
6 *Cows and sheep lie down before rain.*
7 *A cold winter means a hot summer.*
8 *A backing wind which shifts against the sun is a foul wind.*
9 *The moon and the weather change together.*
10 *When mountains and cliffs in the sky appear,*
   Some sudden and violent showers are near.
11 *Cirrus clouds moving in from the south indicate unsettled weather on the way.*
12 *A ring around the moon foretells rain.*
13 *Swallows high, staying dry,*
   Swallows low, wet 'twill blow.
14 *When the leaves show their underside,*
   Be very sure that rain betide.
15 *When the wind is in the east,*
   It bodes no good for man nor beast.
16 *Pine cones clamp up tight and seaweed becomes soft when rain is due.*

17 *Dew before midnight,*
   Tomorrow will be bright.
18 *When the sun sets clear on Wednesday, expect clear weather for*
   the rest of the week.

RELIABILITY RATINGS

1 *False*   When March comes in 'like a lion' (implying storms and lashing gales) it goes out 'like a lamb' (quiet weather, serene winds) only 22 times out of 100. In fact, according to Met Office records there is no better than a fifty-fifty chance that March will open with furious winds and drenching rains; there is just as good a chance that March will 'come in like a lamb and go out like a lion'.

2 *True*   This is one of the best known and most often quoted English weather lores – and with good reason. After 54 recorded sunrise watches when it was raining between the hours of 5 and 9, the day turned out dry by midday on 42 occasions. Ignore the fact that the adage refers to 'seven' and 'eleven'; they are no more than convenient rhyming words which accurately reflect the fact that few rainbelts accompanying a depression last more than four hours.

3 *True*   A word of explanation: rainbows are the result of sun shining through the miniature prisms formed by raindrops, they can only appear opposite the sun and only when the sun is behind the observer, it is impossible to see one in the middle of a summer's day. In the morning, a rainbow can only appear towards the west, and in the evening towards the east – more often in winter than summer.

Because most of Britain's weather travels west to east, it follows that a morning rainbow in the west signifies that rain is approaching from that direction and a shower or two is almost certainly imminent. An evening rainbow in the east, on the other hand, hints that the rainbelt is moving away and that clearer weather will follow.

4 *True*   At first sight this appears to be one of those quaint but dotty countryside sayings about nature's creepy crawlies. There are a lot of them and at least one other blatantly ludicrous froggy dictum, namely,

If frogs instead of appearing yellow, turn russet green then it will presently rain.

This has been proved to be silly because observations show that the only time common frogs change their colouring is as a camouflage to match the appropriate background.

But frog watching on the edge of a swamp in Holland and subsequent observations in England, indicate that the throaty croakings of male frogs increase significantly in volume when rain is not very far away. For the life of me, though, I cannot explain why this should be. I can only hazard a guess that, because frogs cannot tolerate much evaporation of their skin's moisture, they spend periods of dry weather within the water where their croaking is to

'The louder the frog, the more the rain' – an accurate saying

some extent stifled. Before rain, however, when the humidity is higher, they are much more likely to emerge and their croaking therefore becomes more apparent.

As it happens, this adage cannot really be recommended as one of the easy to apply weather lores because too long a time has to be spent harking to frogs before the increase in croaking level becomes apparent.

5 *True* Mackerel skies – those tiny high-flying clouds which gather in fleecy bunches and which some countrymen call 'a curdly sky' or 'flocks of woolly sheep' – omen rain, but generally only in the form of brief and intermittent showers; hence, 'never long wet and never long dry'.

Mackerel skies which were logged during tests, brought rain within twelve hours on 73 occasions out of 103, within 24 hours 87 times out of 103, and within 3 days on 92 occasions out of 103. The good old mackerel sky failed to foretell rain within 72 hours, therefore, on only 4 per cent of test observations.

6 *False* My mother, who was a lovely person with a nature cure for every ill and an appropriate weather saying for every occasion, always warned that rain was on the way when the cattle which grazed our nearby meadows lay down or huddled in disconsolate groups in a corner of the fields. It never occurred to me that she could be wrong.

On reflection, now, it should have done because I doubt if many of her weird and wonderful predictions about the weather were any more successful than her witch-like cures for childish ills. A dirty sock wrapped around my scrawny neck never seemed to speed away a sore throat, while I very much doubt if the rasping cough of a neighbour's daughter was in any way decreased by frequent and nauseating administrations of hot milk steeped in the decomposing body of a dead mouse.

Observations in later years proved that cows are in no

way reliable weather prophets. Cows lay down to chew the cud when it was sunny and destined to stay that way for at least 12 hours, 40 times out of 100; when it was heavily overcast but still failed to rain, 62 times out of 100; and when it was already raining, 67 times out of 100.

'Cows lie down before rain' – an unreliable weather adage

Sheep, I understand from a Sussex farmer, are no better at spotting weather trends and have no greater ability, nor even the sense, to take shelter from the threatening storm. In fact he is sure that sheep are not even intelligent enough to detect when it is actually raining!

7 *False* This is one of the many, many long-term forecasting maxims which promise a lot and yet collapse entirely upon examination. None of the following scored better than a 25 per cent, poor, accuracy rating during researches and one or two, along with their many variations on similar themes, scored even less. So, dismiss as misleading such quaint old sayings as:

> *Onion's skin very thin,*
> *Mild weather coming in;*
> *Onion's skin thick and tough,*
> *Coming winter cold and rough.*

> *A wet spring, a dry harvest,*
> *A dry spring, a raining summer.*

35

A wet summer almost always precedes
   a cold and stormy winter.

Clear autumn, windy winter,
   Warm autumn, long winter.

A serene autumn denotes a windy winter,
   A windy winter a raining spring,
A rainy spring a serene summer,
   A serene summer a windy autumn.

8 *True* The wind is said by some countrymen to go 'withershins', or contrary to the course of the sun, when it 'backs' or shifts in an anti-clockwise direction – for example from north to west. It is always a good general rule that when a strong wind backs, rain is sure to follow.

9 *False* There are so many hundred old weather lores which turn out to be rubbish that it is strange they were coined in the first place, and even more amazing that they have become established as part of our folklore heritage.

   Old men in Suffolk, and no doubt many other places in the British Isles, still quote this one. And only the other day I heard the master of a large freighter predict knowingly *These winds 'll change with the moon.*

   Sadly, the age-old belief, is nonsense. A wiser head than all the rest must have been the first to say;

The moon and weather may change together,
   But change of moon does not change the weather.

He was probably the same chap who added,

If we'd no moon at all,
   And that may seem strange,
We still should have weather
   That's subject to change.

10 *True* The towering heaps of cloud which swell into ominous-looking shower clouds to westward, are a safe bet for wind squalls and rain. But always bear in mind that the rain from banks of shower clouds is almost certainly going to fall over relatively small areas so could pass you by; the wind squalls, though, will be spread over a much wider area. In any case someone, somewhere within the shadow of passing cumulus shower clouds, is going to get wet.

11 *True* – especially during the summer half of the year. Mares'-tail cirrus should be considered the weatherman's cloud, for it is covered by thirty-three different weather lores which reliably predict future winds, rain or fair skies and perfect summer days.

12 *True* One of the few moon sayings which stand up to investigation. A halo round the sun or moon, or milky-yellow haze over either, accurately foretold rain 108 times out 114 logged sightings (95 per cent accuracy).

13 *True* Swallows and swifts fly skywards in order to scoop up the insects which only proceed aloft when the barometer is high or rising and the weather is due to set fair for at least another twenty-four hours or so. They are said to fly low well ahead of a deterioration in the weather because that is when the pressure is falling and the insects on which they feed come down to lower altitudes.

That's the theory, anyway, and half the adage (the bit about flying high, staying dry) appears to be borne out in practice about seven times out of ten. For some reason, though, it is not infallible because, despite whatever the barometer is doing, I have known swallows to appear high in the evening sky, three times out of ten, when rain followed some six hours later. And when they are flying low, rain should be predicted on nothing more than a fifty-fifty basis.

14 *True* This has been intentionally selected because it is one of the most reliable of weather lores relating to trees

– and there are not many of them!

A period of damp air, I am told by botanists, helps to soften the stalks of leaves which then bend more easily in the wind when rain is approaching. My observations were limited to the leaves of Poplar and Sycamore, which seem to turn and twist in a shivering tremble before the coming of worsening weather far more easily than those of other species. I have no doubt, though, that the lore may be just as successfully applied to other types of trees.

15 *True* During the winter, some of Britain's most bitter-cold weather comes on an east or north-east wind. Given a falling barometer as well, an easterly promises a storm brewing up.

16 *False* – despite the generations of small boys and big dads who have taken seaweed home in the belief that it will turn soft when rain is due and become stiff and dry when the sun is due to shine. In fact, as far as my bit of seaweed is concerned, it turned stiff as a board once well away from the coast and stayed that way forever more – come rain or shine.

As for pine cones, the ones upon my bulkhead shelf have remained open for the past six months despite the rains which have lashed from time to time during that period.

But I am sure that day-trippers will still take seaweed from the beach, and wanderers in the pine woods will continue to pocket cones. And why not?

17 *True* The ancient Greeks believed that Eos, goddess of dawn, shed tears at sunrise and so sprinkled the world with dew. In fact on calm, near-windless nights in summer, when there are clear skies and the air is moist and clean, the goddess begins to weep long before the sun clears the eastern horizon. Dew before midnight signals a 99·9 per cent chance of a fair day tomorrow; my records tempt me to predict a 100 per cent certainty, but I have grown wary – as you will – of any weather forecast which smacks of the absolute.

38

Dewless nights in summer do not indicate the probability of rain next day, so I recommend you seek out other omens.

18 *True* I would have put money on this one turning out a complete flop. Weather records – not mine, but those of the official, pukka-scientific met man – show that a clear sunset on Wednesday is likely to be followed by dry, settled weather until, at least, the following weekend, six times out of ten. Logically, it should have proved no better than a fifty-fifty chance one way or the other. I love it when logic is put to the run.

Chapter Four

COMPLEXION OF THE SKY

It's easy to crib from Shakespeare:

Men judge by the complexion of the sky, the state and inclination of the day. (King Richard II, 3, 2).

And it would be just as simple to crib from two dozen or so academic works on meteorological science in order to expound with grand pomposity on the factors which make our weather the fickle fool that it is. I shall resist the temptation, partly because I do not properly comprehend the cauldron froth of events within which our weather system is created, and partly because I am fairly sure the meteorological expert does not understand it very much better.

In any case I am convinced that it matters not a jot. I know, from personal experience, that it is unnecessary to delve into weather science in order to predict with some degree of accuracy the approach of rain, wind or sun over a single local area. I also know, that meteorology can be an arduous and frustrating study of this and that, of invisible fronts and never-to-be-seen air masses, of the troposphere and katabatic winds and goodness only knows what else besides. For all those brave and enquiring souls who must know exactly what causes the weather to act the screwball way it does, the public library is full of specialised volumes. For the rest of us, it is fully possible to forecast local weather simply by keeping an eye on changes taking place in the sky. It helps, of course, to look out for other natural signs as well, such as air-pressure changes indicated by the activities of birds or plants and reliably registered by the barometer: but most of all it is vital to detect sky signs.

The weather which reaches the British Isles is no more than the end result of the world's air in perpetual motion, a capricious swirl of scattiness which is the bane of forecasters. Only when meteorologists are able to expand convincingly upon that fact, will their studies approach something close to an exact science. At present, their jargon-laden pronouncements amount to little more than the bare-bones business of our weather – that winds change, and grow stronger or diminish, clouds gather and disperse, rain falls or turns to snow or hail and the sun shines. They know, by and large, how these phenomena happen; they still don't know very much about why or where.

BLUE SKIES

Never trust a clear blue sky,
Even if the glass points high.

Reliability rating: excellent. It would be easy to dismiss this couplet as hopelessly pessimistic or unnecessarily gloomy; after all, only a real putty-head would batten down the hatches and haul oilskins from dark recesses merely because the sky is clear blue all the way to the horizon. On face value, the adage is worth no more than a reluctantly awarded 'good'; but as a warning never to trust any sky it rates the highest possible mark. Never automatically trust any sky; keep a lookout for possible weather-change signs all the time. Become a 'gloomy-Joe' if you must, although it is as well to keep your cheerless melancholia a dark secret from those nearest, dearest and longest suffering.

And, as the couplet implies, never implicitly trust the barometer either – especially just because it is registering high, low or somewhere in the middle. Where the needle rests at any one time nearly always means very little or even nothing; by and large, it is the rate of rise and fall which counts (see Chapter 14).

As a matter of proven fact, blue skies do not invariably presage continued swimsuit weather. It is surprising just how soon fine, golden days can turn to depressing grey if they have a mind to. A steel-blue sky, in fact, is only crystal clear because there are few dust particles in the air – a state of affairs hinting that rain may not be very far over the horizon. But do not be depressed. Look on the bright side and predict that the weather will continue fine; there's an excellent chance that you will be right. Nevertheless, keep taking regular rain and wind checks throughout the day, and always keep in mind all the time that

> *A dark, gloomy-blue sky is a windy*
> *one which warns of rain,*
> *But light, bright blue means gentle*
> *breezes and fair weather is stayin'.*

Reliability rating: good for the first line, excellent for the second. I once knew a lovable old crackpot who always lugged two vital items of stores on board before slipping his mooring for a summer-day sailabout – a crate of beer which, he would lisp through toothless gums, 'will souse the inner man, fetch rose buds to me cheeks, and get me pissed', and an enormous golfing umbrella with which to protect his bald head if the blue sky turned to rain. He believed wholeheartedly, you see, in the lore that dark-blue morning skies invariably turn to rain before nightfall. The rest of the world believed he was bonkers.

In fact, he was, a bit. But it now seems likely that he would have needed that umbrella three times out of ten when the mid-morning sky was an over-dark, steely blue,

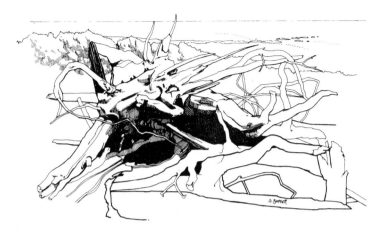

Sloppy winds and a cobweb blue sky – a good day for mooching along the tide line

for my records show that a steel-blue sky turns to rain before nightfall 31 times out of 138 occasions; not anything like a reliable accuracy rating, it is true, but it does go to prove that you cannot automatically trust dark-blue skies.

Light, bright-blue skies are a different matter entirely, promising fine weather for at least the remainder of the day, and winds which can range from complete calm to around Force 4. The gusts depend on the amount and type of cloud about, but in tests they never exceeded Force 5 whenever there was at least 80 per cent clear sky.

So, if the sky is a hard, dark blue, forecast moderate to fresh winds and a possible chance of rain towards the butt-end of the day. For gentle, light-blue skies predict winds which will probably blow somewhere between calm and light (not forgetting, though, there is always a 30 per cent possibility of them becoming moderate or even fresh) with only a slim possibility of rain. In fact there is a better than 90 per cent chance that the weather will remain dry for twelve hours at least.

> *When as much blue is seen in the sky as will make a*
> *pair of sailor's trousers, the weather will improve.*

Reliability rating: very good, providing the adage is applied after the gloom of a depression (see page 121). Bear in mind, though, that the improvement will almost certainly carry with it the threat of showers and could well be only a temporary break before the approach of another bad-weather front.

If the blue patches noticeably increase, there is an excellent chance that the weather will get significantly better over the next twelve hours; winds will fall to Force 2–3, probably veering.

GLOOMY SKIES, GLOOMY DAY

> *The approach of a warm front with its drizzle, the*
> *gradual backing of the wind against the sun and an*
> *increase in velocity, together with that murky and*
> *strangely translucent greyness all round, typifies the*
> *path of a depression.*

Reliability rating: excellent. This is not one of your old-time weather sayings, but is an exceedingly valuable observation for all that. It was made in his book, *Cruising*, by that excellent author on all matters to do with the sea and small boats, J. D. (Des) Sleightholme, former editor of *Yachting Monthly*. The observation provides all the indicators of an imminent warm front which is the first bad-weather feature of a depression.

It is recognition of that 'murky and strangely translucent greyness all round' which, together with a falling barometer, marks the approach of a low. Once accurately identified it is possible to forecast with 90 per cent accuracy that winds will increase, bringing with them a risk of some very strong gusts; rain which is only minutes away (and could, in fact, already be falling); and a significant fall in temperature. For full details on predicting a depression see Chapter 13.

> *A grey and featureless sky*
> *May be a gloomy one,*
> *But at least it's dry.*

Reliability rating: excellent, providing you get the identification factors right. It must be a 'featureless' sheet of unbroken grey sky, often stretching from horizon to horizon. Importantly, there must be no hint of any contoured shape about the gloomy cloud layer.

The other sort of low-level grey sheet, the one which presages wind and wet, is also a dark cloud layer which stretches right across the sky. But this time, instead of being an unbroken smear of cloud it contains clearly identifiable grey-mauve elements jumbled within it in ragged and vaguely outlined shapes. It is a chaos of low-level rain-clouds, scrambled within a stratus formation, which bring with them lingering spells of heavy rain and/or drizzle.

Forecast dry weather when the low-altitude cloud sheet is a featureless mass; predict rain when it is stirred into a closely mingled mass of individual elements.

GREEN SKY

> *If the sky in rainy weather is tinged with sea-green, the rain will stay.*

Reliability rating: good, until the observer has become accustomed to spotting the correct shade of green which is usually seen as no more than a brush-stroke of colour along the base of a heavy cloud layer. Once you know exactly what you're looking for, the reliability rating is upgraded to excellent.

In all honesty the adage is really not a lot of use because

any sign of green in the sky never occurs unless it is either raining already or there is so much rain in the sky that only an incurable optimist would ignore its threat. But it does enable the weather watcher to predict with confidence a further and prolonged fall of rain or showers, which is little more than minutes away.

YELLOW SKY

A dirty yellow sky indicates likelihood of increasing wind and rain from the south-west or west – especially if accompanied by, first, a backing, and later a veering, wind.

Reliability rating: excellent, but only if the trace of yellow is undoubtedly grubby looking – more like the yellowish creamy white identified in the next adage – and is accompanied by a wind which after backing veers towards the south-west. The chances of the saying proving correct are increased considerably if the barometer shows signs of falling at the same time.

If the sky seems washed with creamy white,
The rain is near though not yet in sight.

Reliability factor: excellent. If it wasn't for a problem of rhyming, I suspect the originator of this couplet would have described the wash as 'creamy yellow' rather than 'creamy white'.

The first really reliable sky-sign warning of an approaching depression comes when high-flying clouds thicken and slowly lower to become a yellowish, creamy-white mid-altitude layer across the whole sky. The sun, first only thinly veiled by a sky-borne mist, disappears almost completely to become little more than a blurred haze of golden light. This is the first true hint that a depression is on the way, and is usually confirmed by a falling barometer and winds that back and veer.

Predict a nine times out of ten chance of continuous, moderate rainfall within two to four hours (likely to last, off and on, for something like twenty hours) and winds which increase – often to as much as Force 5–6 in the summer and Force 6–7 in the winter – over the coming four to six hours.

RAINBOWS

My heart leaps up when I behold,
ʼ   A rainbow in the sky.
(William Wordsworth)

A few basic facts about rainbows should be noted. Remember, a rainbow can only appear when the sun is behind the observer's back. One seen towards the east indicates that the rain is moving away, one appearing in the western sky promises a good chance of rain falling soon. It is possible to get some idea of just how much rain by the colour of a rainbow: the heavier the rain, the more vivid the hues. Fine drizzle produces a general fading of the colours – red, orange, yellow, green, blue, indigo and violet – all contained in the mnemonic, Richard Of York Gave Battle In Vain.

The following rainbow saws should be heeded.

If the rainbow forms and disappears suddenly, there will be serene and settled weather soon.

When a rainbow is formed in an approaching cloud expect a shower; in a receding cloud, fine weather.

A rainbow in the evening means fair weather during the coming night.

If the colours of a rainbow are faded and barely discernible, fair weather is on the way very soon.

'Rainbow to windward, foul falls the day' – accurate seven times out of ten

Rainbow to windward, foul falls the day,
Rainbow to leeward, damp runs away.

When the outside colour of the rainbow is noticeably red
rather than orange, rain will be heavy; when the red
and orange bands are weak, the amount of rain will be
small.

48

If blue predominates the colours of a rainbow, the weather is clearing.

> *If rainbow green is large and bright,*
> *Rain is still somewhere in sight;*
> *If red is strongest colour of all,*
> *Then winds will blow, rains will fall.*

Reliability rating: Good for all the adages; average accuracy about seven out of ten.

SUN HALO

A halo round the sun appears before rain.

Reliability rating: good for rain within 24 hours, excellent, though, as a longer term 48-hour forecast. A halo is a bright circle appearing around the sun or moon. In fact, it is far easier to see one around the moon because the glare from the sun very often virtually snuffs it out.

In practice, the chances of rain following the appearance of a halo within 24 hours worked out at just less than seven times out of ten. There was an astonishingly impressive probability rating of 95 per cent for rain within 48 hours. So count on a halo foretelling rain, and almost certainly higher winds, at least within 2 days' time.

MOCK SUN

Mock sun, dry on the run.

Reliability rating: no better than average to poor. Reckon on a mock sun presaging rain on a fifty-fifty basis. In fact you might just as well toss a coin, but it does provide a warning that a threat of rain is in the air.

A mock sun, by the way, is just what it says it is – a brightly coloured sun spot, an imitation of the real thing, seen in the clouds about level with the proper sun.

Chapter Five

SIGHT, SOUND AND SNIFF

There are, I understand, several reasons why sounds should travel faster and farther, and distant objects appear clearer and closer than normal, when there is a threat of rain and gales in the air. It is all to do with such matters as temperature inversion and air humidity, and the fact that winds increase in speed the higher they are from the ground.

The following sight, sound and sniff adages have, to one degree or another, generally proved to be reliable weather portents.

SIGHT

The farther the sight, the nearer the rain.

Reliability rating: good, but would be worthy of a much better rating if it was always easy to determine the difference between a normally clear day in summer and an exceptionally clear one that forebodes rain. Generally speaking, if distant objects appear abnormally closer than they actually are, it pays to predict the *possibility* of rain within six to eight hours.

Personally, I have only got the forecast right on about a fifty-fifty basis; but I think I still have to learn how to identify an exceptional 'seeing day'. Many working boatmen I know seem to get a much better reliability rating.

Cornish fishermen working their pots and nets around the Manacles say,

> *When the Lizard is clear,*
> *Rain is near.*

Sussex boatmen working off southern beaches maintain,

> *When the Isle of Wight is seen from Brighton or*
> *Worthing, expect rain soon.*

In a Kentish pub I once heard a Dover local say,

> *When you see the whites of a Frenchman's eye, then rain*
> *is on the doorstep of old England.*

So it seems that variations on 'the farther the sight, the nearer the rain' are rules of thumb which countless generations of seamen have relied on. I shall keep testing it, but do not expect it ever to prove as reliable as

> *When the scape looks clear with your back to the sun*
> *expect fine weather, but when it looks clear with your*
> *face towards the sun then expect showery, unsettled*
> *weather.*

Reliability rating: very good – more than 80 per cent accuracy; and a much more workable, and therefore more reliable, refinement of the preceding maxims.

> *Haze is a sign of stable weather.*

Reliability rating: excellent. This is the reverse of

> *A hard, clear horizon is a sign of wet weather*

and all the other aforementioned clear-day weather maxims.

Whenever a summer day is hazy, confidently predict

51

that the weather will stay dry, and probably fine, for at least the next twelve hours. During tests, a hazy day was followed by dry weather for twenty-four hours, seven times out of ten.

Smoke rising vertically is a sign of settled weather; when it descends upon house roofs and passes along the eaves expect rain and wind within six hours.

Reliability rating: very good for the first part if, in these days of clean-air bills, you can get sight of a smoking chimney. A bonfire will do, as will the horrifying gaseous-yellow smoke from one of the power-station chimneys which scar our estuaries.

Certainly, when smoke rises vertically it is safe to make a nine to one bet on a full twenty-four hours of fine skies and gentle winds – so gentle on many summer mornings, in fact, that it might pay sail-boat skippers to dawdle at anchor for a while or switch on the engine. The wind should pick up, though, during the day.

I cannot vouch for the latter part of the saying. There are just not enough smoking chimneys about these days to form a proper judgement on what smoke descending on the roof and curling along the eaves foretells.

SOUND

A good hearing day is a sign of wet.

Reliability rating: very good and quite a lot better than the good-sight portents. Perhaps, of course, I've got more reliable ears than eyes.

Faint sounds heard from far-distant places on calm days – especially during a temporary fair-weather lull after rain – promise that the weather will not remain settled long. The maxim, though, is not to be relied upon at night, when distant sounds and continuing dry conditions appear to go hand in hand.

A murmuring, which some folk call a roar, heard in a wood although there is no big wind beyond the trees, is a sign of wind and rain approaching the land.

Reliability rating: a tentative very good, although observations have been too few and far between to really justify such a lordly marking.

When I lived in the south-west of England my footpath to the sea passed through a coppice of Sycamores and Elms. I was consciously aware of a 'murmuring' in the trees, when there was no wind to speak of outside the plantation, on just two occasions. On one, it was followed later in the day by a big wind from the south-west which swept a lash of rain towards the cliffs. The other time, the morning grew slowly more overcast until a typical Cornish summer mizzle was brushed on gentle breezes, from out of the sea.

SNIFF

When ditches, drains or the midden heap stink something evil, there's rain in the air for sure.

Reliability rating: very good, and a reminder that old countrymen actually did sniff out the weather. According to my nose, when ditches, drains and the dung heap of a midden yard (not so common these days except around riding stables) reek more foully than normal, there is a 78 per cent chance – call it eight times out of ten – of rain within ten hours.

People with a reputation to maintain as weather prophets tend to sniff the wind a good deal. It doesn't do any good, but it has become expected of them. The few friends among fishermen of Cornwall that an invader from up-country, such as I, could establish, have been doing it as a tourist attraction for years. I recommend that you develop the habit for it will help wonderfully in fostering –

When the stableyard midden heap appears to smell more than normal, there's rain in the air for sure

at least amongst those nearest and dear – a mystical ability on your part to read invisible messages which are carried upon the wind.

One or two fishermen who have refined their performances to something of an art form, purse their lips, too, and suck knowingly upon their teeth before shaking a dubious head at the skies and flopping away on deep-sea boots to the safety of a harbour bar. Some have not left that bar for more than an occasional wind-sniff for several seasons. You need not go to such lengths. Merely sniff the wind. It is enough.

Chapter Six

GREASE BALLS AND
WOOLLY FLEECES

From towering grey dreadnoughts to unpredictable little blimps, clouds are not to be trusted. Even a comparatively little one, looking as friendly as you like, could be lugging around something like 1,000 tons of atmosphere and all manner of unexpected debris besides. Storm clouds once deposited barrow-loads of crabs and periwinkles onto the streets of a North American town which lies a good 40 miles (64 km) from the nearest sea and should, therefore, be safe from any such invasion.

Whether they are bombing the earth with sea food, sending squalls which lay sail-boats flat to their scuppers, or merely brushing gentle tendrils of wind across the heads of tall grasses, clouds present an ever-changing skyscape of infinite, fascinating variety.

It is not easy to reach a proper understanding of their fickle nature without swotting up descriptions of individual cloud characteristics and memorising a listing of Latin tags. At best, it's an off-putting chore. For ages I rejected the Latin names with studied eccentricity, persisting exclusively with the word-pictures of our forefathers: hen scarts, mackerel skies, cauliflower heads and so on. It was a romantically imposed rejection of things smacking of the scientific.

Sadly, it didn't work, largely because the old people did not have an appropriate nickname for many cloud formations, and partly because the Latin names used in reference works did not always have an old-English world-picture equivalent.

It is possible, however, to get a reliable general guide to cloud portents with the aid of a rough-and-ready glance at some of grandfather's best cloud observations.

GREASE BALLS

Hard-edged grease-ball clouds are bad-weather breeders.

Cloudy, greasy skies generally foretell southerly, south-west and south-east breezes – especially when there is a cold and misty feel about the air.

Reliability rating: very good for the first adage, good for the second. Any cloud which has a hard, jagged edge threatens poorer weather in the form of wind squalls and/or rain. So, too, do any skies which appear to have been coated in a thin film of grease.

The second adage, which foretells winds from a southern quarter, has proved reliable between six and seven times out of ten.

WOOLLY FLEECES

If woolly fleeces strew the heavenly way,
  Be sure no rain disturbs the summer day.

Cotton waifs are fair-weather flyers.

Reliability ratings: excellent. These are just a couple of the dozen or so old weather-lore sayings which refer to the soft and cushiony clouds associated with fine weather. The first is taken from one of the earliest books entirely devoted to weather lores – *Shepherd of Banbury's Rules to Judge the Changes of the Weather*, published in 1744 and written by John Claridge who was probably this Banbury, Oxfordshire, shepherd. There are twenty-six rules in all and the best, the reliable, appear throughout these pages;

a very few proved plain daft during observation tests.

Woolly fleeces or cotton waifs, more often referred to these days as fair-weather cumulus, always accompany blue skies and settled weather which can be relied upon to stay that way for at least a day or so. More on cumulus clouds in Chapter 7, meanwhile remember that

Fair-weather clouds are good humoured.

Reliability rating: excellent. Indeed, they are – good-tempered, dry-weather, cumulus bundles with podgy heads of cotton-wool and clearly defined flat bases.

HIGH CLOUDS
High skies, high clouds are generally fair-weather omens.

Reliability rating: excellent A high sky – even one which slowly clouds over and gives clear warning of an approaching depression (see Chapter 13) – usually remains dry, even though the weather may turn from fine to poor, for at least twelve hours.

As a general rule any high cloud formation usually accompanies set-fine weather unless the sky begins to thicken over and the cloudbase lowers perceptibly (see next adage).

LOWERING SKIES
Low'rin clouds, low'rin skies,
Stay indoors if you are wise.

Reliability rating: very good. A lowering sky which develops out of a steadily thickening layer of higher cloud indicates that unsettled weather with increasing winds and threat of rain is imminent.

CLOUD BENCH

A bench of clouds in the west means fine weather or it means rain or it don't mean nothing at all.

Reliability rating: nil. I have repeated this saying exactly the way it was told me by a really objectionable old fisherman who used to sponge on tourists for beer in a Cornish pub, and who sent a spittle of cackles across the protruding plate of his false teeth, as he said it. His triple alternatives graphically illustrate the fact that a bench, or bank, of clouds which can often be seen on the horizon, does not predict the good weather which some of the old saws would have us believe it does. Nor does it foretell rain. It is, in fact, a sign of absolutely no significance at all.

SPOTTED SKY

If the sky, from being clear, becomes fretted all over with cloud, rain and new winds are likely within the space of half a day.

The cloud formation referred to is what mariners have become accustomed to calling a 'mackerel sky' because it looks very much like the scales of that fish. Another saw on the same theme has already been referred to:

> *Mackerel sky, mackerel sky,*
> *Never long wet, never long dry.*

Reliability rating: excellent. As I wrote earlier (page 34), mackerel skies omen showers within at least three days' time. When, however, a generally clear blue sky becomes quickly fretted all over with mackerel cloud then rain, and almost certainly a brisker wind, is 70 per cent probable within six hours or so.

EARTH CLOUDS

Earth clouds fly ahead of worsening weather.

Reliability rating: very good. It was something of a struggle to decide just what type of cloud this adage refers to. After much head scratching I opted for the dark, heavy clouds which scuttle along beneath a low and overcast layer of gloomy stratus. They are often so low to the ground that they can fairly be described as 'earth clouds', which reliably warn of unsettled weather with fresh to strong winds and drenching rain.

I once heard this form of sky called 'a mucky mess'. It's a fair description.

HIGH CLOUD SHEET

A cap of sheet cloud high in the sky,
Forewarns the tears from heaven's eye.

Reliability rating: doubtful. This is a warning of a typical bad-weather front approaching: a high sheet of cloud which slowly covers the sun with a veil of mist before thickening still further and lowering not long ahead of rain and a freshening wind.

The adage, however, is far from infallible and it should never be assumed that a thin veil across the sun or moon automatically heralds the coming of a depression. Observation of associated barometer and wind trends will help provide a surer guide to the sort of weather on the way (see Chapter 14).

GATHERING CLOUDS

When clouds are gathering thick and fast,
Keep a lookout for sails and mast;
But if they slowly onward crawl,
Shoot your nets, line, trawls and all.

'When mountains and cliffs in the clouds appear, some sun and violent showers are near'

Reliability rating: good. This saying comes from the East Coast and neatly sums up the portents of gathering clouds. It should be treated as no better than a warning; a great deal depends on the type of cloud formation (see Chapters 6–8). For all that, it is a useful reminder of a general tendency for the weather to deteriorate when the sky collects clouds.

FEATHERING CLOUDS

When the clouds spread like a feather,
Mariners look for fair, good weather.

Reliability rating: very good generally speaking, if strong winds in the upper regions of the sky brush the clouds into feathery trails before whisking them away entirely, there is little chance of any major weather deterioration. The same applies to aircraft vapour trails: when they persist in the sky the weather is almost certain to change for the worse, if they quickly shred, the good weather will remain.

MOUNTAINOUS CLOUDS

When mountains and cliffs in the clouds appear,
Some sun and violent showers are near.

Reliability rating: excellent. Towering clouds which rise out of cottony heaps and develop into huge masses, often produce heavy showers and brief sunny periods. It is worth noting that

The deeper the cloud,
The harder it showers.

BLACK CLOUDS

Towering black clouds with rounded tops warn of thunder and squalls.

Reliability rating: very good. All black clouds do not automatically threaten thunder or wind squalls, but it makes good sense to suspect them of doing so. At sea, keep an eye on the water beneath any approaching black beastie for signs of wind on the waves.

BLACK SHEEP

If a flock of greyish-black sheep clouds appear in the north-western sky towards sunset, it will rain before the next day.

Reliability rating: excellent. This is a precise description of what is, in actual fact, a fairly unusual occurrence. It did prove to be fully reliable on the handful of occasions I was able to put it to the test.

ANVIL CLOUDS

Anvil clouds carry wind and rain with them.

Reliability rating: excellent. A cloud shaped like a blacksmith's anvil developing at the summit of a towering wool-pack cloud, gives timely warning of heavy rain and wind squalls.

CLEARING SKY

When clouds leave the sky it is an omen of fair weather.

Reliability rating: very good. This saying is so obvious that it barely seems worthy of inclusion. Still, it does provide a reminder that a sky which clears after a period of poor weather normally promises a general improvement.

HILL CAPS

Clouds which cap hills forbode rain.

Reliability rating: fair. Misty clouds which form or hang over hills do, indeed, indicate that wind and rain is likely. But if they gradually disperse there is an 83 per cent chance that the weather will remain dry and could, in fact, improve substantially.

RULES OF THUMB

Clear, light-blue skies are bearers of fine weather and light breezes.

Clear, steel-blue skies often stay generally fine but nevertheless provide a hint that deteriorating weather and fresher winds are possible.

Hard-edged clouds presage wind squalls and very often bring rain.

Soft clouds promise continuing settled weather with gentle moderate winds.

Reliability rating: excellent, for these very generalised rules of thumb which I drew up as a personal guide in my initial days as a weather spotter. Some dozen years later they still hold good as a summary of many old weather lores.

By and large, rules of thumb for cloud spotting are no substitute for the real thing – the nitty-gritty, brass-tacks cloud lore. But that requires identification of at least some of the cloud elements in the sky and, even with a list of guidelines, such as those I try to provide in Chapters 7 and 8, proper identification is about as easy as picking out, say, a Geordie from a Scouse by the shape of his head. The skies are often such a mess, such a jumble of various elements just about anybody can spot a perfect textbook example of, say, an altostratus sky, but scramble it up with various other bits and pieces, and identification is nowhere quite so easy.

Don't let it worry you. And don't be confused by any jargon of *altocumulus castellanus floccus,* and what have you. Just get the very basic cloud formations straight in your mind's eye and the weather lores will take care of the rest. I no longer worry over much about chaotic jumbled, all-sorts skies, but merely strive to pick out what appears to be the most conspicuous element or elements and apply the appropriate weather lores. In any case, if the sky is truly chaotic you can be pretty sure that something peculiar and generally nasty is on the way.

The following is probably the most useful, the most reliable, of all cloud lores. It is important enough to be called 'Prime cloud lore', and should be applied at every available opportunity.

PRIME CLOUD LORE

By standing with your back to the surface wind and observing which way the upper clouds are moving, it is possible to tell just what the weather will do: improve, deteriorate or continue almost exactly as it is.

Reliability rating: excellent. There are many sound, scientific reasons why this lore is able to achieve just what it promises. Go out half a dozen times or so and prove to yourself that it provides a true and accurate guide to the weather. The procedure is as follows:

1 Stand with your back to the wind and, if the upper clouds are moving from your left to right hand, the weather will deteriorate nine times out of ten.
2 Stand with your back to the wind and, if the upper clouds are moving from your right to left hand, the weather will improve nine times out of ten.
3 Stand with your back to the wind and, if the upper clouds are moving on a parallel course, the weather will not change greatly seven times out of ten.

Strictly speaking, the wind you are feeling on your back is not the true wind, which is generally that being followed by the lower clouds such as cumulus, stratocumulus and so on. What you are actually trying to do is judge in which direction the upper clouds (the ones nearest the sky ceiling) are moving in relation to the lower ones; in practice it is not always easy to do that by eye. So the best and easiest way of putting the lore into operation is by locating the direction of the true lower wind, through rotating 10 degrees clockwise after establishing the direction of the surface wind on your back at sea, and 30 degrees clockwise over land. Then judge the directional drift of the upper clouds.

Note that the above rules only apply in the northern hemisphere. In the southern hemisphere it is necessary to stand facing the wind.

Chapter Seven

MARES' TAILS AND MACKEREL SCALES

Two factors decide just what cloud is what, and the group to which it belongs – shape and height. Basically there are three distinctive shapes:

1 Cumuloform: cotton-wool 'pile' or 'heap' clouds which are typified by the fair-weather puff-balls frequently depicted in childrens' paintings; they range from individual plump wodges to massive banks of towering cauliflower heads.

2 Stratiform: the grubby 'layer' or 'spread out' clouds which provide the British Isles with what we disparagingly claim is our typical overcast and gloomy sky.

3 Cirroform: the wispish 'lock of hair' or 'tendril' clouds which seamen have long known as 'mares' tails'.

These are the three basic formations; there are no others. Now for the distinctive heights at which, in one form or another, they appear.

The very highest clouds of all, with bases ranging somewhere between 16,000ft (5km) and 45,000ft (14km) from the ground, are cirroform. They can appear in three different forms:

1 White scratchings of mares'-tail elements known officially as 'cirrus'.

65

2 Closer and more consolidated as a speckle of tiny white puff-balls which are officially called 'cirrocumulus' but are more lovingly regarded as 'mackerel sky'.

3 Spread out into a thin smear of cream-yellow mist which faintly veils the sun and moon and is called 'cirrostratus'.

Lose height and we reach the middle-level clouds – the 'alto elements'. Take a bundle of cumulus cotton-wool clouds, arrange them into a neat and closely spaced formation, put them on the middle-height deck of between 7,000 and 25,000ft (2–8km) and they become altocumulus – distinguishable from a ceiling-high cirrocumulus mackerel sky only by virtue of the fact that, because they are that much lower, the shading of each individual element is clearly apparent.

Now spread the altocumulus formation out into a welded middle-height layer of cloud and it becomes altostratus. Shove some individual, and preferably dirty-grey near-black, clouds into the middle of that lot and you have nimbostratus.

Finally, there is the low-level group – any clouds with a base less than 7,000ft (2km) from the ground. There are four of them:

1 Cumulus: white cotton-wool elements which either come in individual form or packaged into banks.

2 Cumulonimbus: swollen lumps of white, grey and even grubby-black cumulus piles which actually look as if they are overloaded with water vapour – which they are!

3 Stratus: a more or less featureless grey-white sheet which looms gloomy and appears to threaten rain but which, surprisingly, does

not always turn, as the met men say, 'to precipitation'.

4 Stratocumulus: a jumbled mass of cumulus bits and pieces which have become scrambled into a grey-white low stratus layer.

In broad terms, that's it. Now to look closely at the highest altitude formations and at the similar altocumulus, and see the sort of weather they bring.

CIRRUS (Ci)

It is useful to start off any weather lore listing of the clouds with cirrus (Ci in meteorological shorthand). For one thing it's the cloud on top of the pile; for another, it is probably one of the easiest to identify. Finally, and most importantly, it provides some of the most detailed and accurate weather sayings of all.

High-level, thin Ci cloud consists of ice crystals – and looks it. It is the ice and low temperatures up near the roof of the sky which give basic cirrus such a light, very fine and delicate appearance, resembling tendrils of hair or the light feather strokes of zinc-white paint from an artist's brush.

Old countrymen used to call Ci formations 'goat's hair', 'curly wisps' or 'fillies' tails'. It is probably because cirrus normally trails a distinctive hook-flick that seamen for generations have referred to it as mares' tails.

> *Thickening cirrus clouds, particularly when they jet stream in dense trails across the sky, promise rain and fresh winds within six to eight hours and provide early warning of the deteriorating weather of an approaching low-pressure warm front.*

Reliability rating: excellent. This can't, however, be considered one of the old weather lores. It is, rather, an

Thickening cirrus clouds provide early warning of an approaching depression and high winds

accumulated potage of all the advice on cirrus contained in just about every book on meteorology I have been able to lay my hands on. It forms the kernel of what they all promised, and so seemed worthy of putting to the test.

A word or two, first, on what the lore implies. When cirrus thickens and gradually invades more and more of the sky, then rain and freshening winds should be prepared for. The faster it thickens and the more of the sky it invades, the sooner the bad-weather front will reach you, typically bringing fresh winds and rain within about six to eight hours.

The promise of rain and fresh within six to eight hours did not stand up to tests so well as I had hoped. In fact, rain followed behind thickening cirrus in less than 12 hours on 270 occasions out of 501 recorded – about 60 per cent of the time. But the longer the time gap allowed, the better the chances: rain within 36 hours, 85 per cent of the time; rain within 72 hours, 95 per cent.

Results like that must qualify cirrus cloud for an 'excellent' rating, despite the time lag necessary before it gets as high as a nine out of ten marking. Bear in mind, though, that it applies only for thick cirrus; a tendril or two of mares' tails is not enough and signifies, in fact, very little at all.

There is one way of working out the chances of cirrus turning to rain with fresh or even strong winds:

> *When cirrus thickens and then turns to a milky sheet of yellowish-white – sometimes accompanied by a halo round the sun – there is a 75 per cent chance of rain within twelve hours. When the sky lowers still further to a featureless middle-deck altostratus sheet, sometimes accompanied by wool-pack cumulus, there is an 87 per cent chance of rain within six hours (sometimes as soon as two hours) and strong winds an hour or so later.*

Again, this is not a truly long-established weather lore, although many generations of seadogs and farmers have passed down the bare-bones principles in one form or another. It is another attempt to establish a set of reliable weather predictions based on personal observation, a lifetime of experience, and picking the brains of other, more knowledgeable, seamen. You will discover that it is no more than the initial stages of cloud development in front of a depression (see Chapter 13).

> *Mares' tail clouds at great height accompanied by a steady barometer denotes fair weather.*

Reliability rating: excellent. Given high-flying cirrus (and, as it so happens, any cumulus clouds) with a steady barometer (near, say, the 1012.5mb or 29.90 inches mark), fair weather can be counted on.

> *Mares' tails, mares' tails,*
> *Make tall ships carry low sails.*

Reliability rating: doubtful. It produced a mixed bag of results in tests scoring, on average, no better than five out of ten, and would normally have been discarded in the waste bin had it not been for the fact that it is one of the best loved, most famous of adages and is still quoted by sailors. It deserves, therefore, at least a mention, but only to discount, hopefully once and for all, the rhyme's implied reliability.

Some mares' tail clouds – those that cover a goodly proportion of the sky, or those thin and wispy formations of Ci which are accompanied by backing or westerly winds (especially when the barometer is falling) – do produce strong winds – 51 per cent of them within 1 day, 72 per cent in 2 days, 81 per cent in 3 days. Some, the ones that form no more than thin wisps in the sky, do not – unless they become gradually dense enough to rate as thick cirrus. In fact, there is one old lore which categorically states:

> *Thin tracings in the sky with painter's brush,*
> *Never expect winds round you rush.*

A reverend Victorian gentleman, Clement Ley, spent a good many off-duty hours watching the skies. The results of his detailed observations deserve to be much better known, because my own tests confirm that they are to be relied upon. All the sayings which conclude this section on cirrus came originally from his pen. They are worthy of, on average, a 70 per cent reliability marking.

Cirrus from SE

> *Cirrus moving from the south-east is almost invariably followed by thunder with damp and sultry weather in the summer. In winter it indicates fine weather except when occurring immediately after heavy rain when it is commonly followed by squalls.*

Cirrus from S

> *Cirrus moving from the south indicates:*
> *1 showery weather in summer when accompanied by a fairly low barometer and after a fall of rain;*
> *2 thunderstorms in summer when accompanied by a high barometer;*
> *3 rough, squally weather in winter when the barometer is fairly low;*
> *4 a sign of favourable weather in winter when accompanied by a high barometer.*

Cirrus from SW

> *Cirrus moving from the south-west often precedes moderately fine weather in summer but can indicate thunderstorms. In winter weather will be unsettled and sometimes stormy.*

Cirrus from W

> *Cirrus moving from the west indicates fine weather in the warm months of the year. In winter it is a symptom of unsettled weather.*

71

Cirrus from NW

> *Cirrus moving from the north-west is bad; in particular when it occurs just after a rise in the barometer when the glass is likely to fall again suddenly and wind and rain will follow.*

Cirrus from WNW–NW

> *Cirrus from anywhere between west-north-west and north-west, especially with rapid cloud movement, is always followed by unsettled weather.*

Reliability rating: good to very good, all scoring, on average, a marking of 77 per cent.

CIRROCUMULUS (Cc)

This is the true mackerel sky: puffy, high cumulus clouds which, because they occur so high from the earth, appear quite tiny and are usually arranged across the sky in parallel rippled layers. It is the sky which is easily confused with the lower, and therefore much bigger, rippled puffs of altocumulus. As it happens, the confusion doesn't much matter because both cloud formations give an equal chance of rain (see comments on mackerel and alto cumulus skies, pages 34 and 73).

Cirrocumulus clouds are often seen in good weather when winds are light to moderate. Unless Cc starts to lower gradually in altitude it is usually nothing to worry about – merely a promise of further good sailing breezes. It's when mackerel skies start to thicken and get progressively lower and lower that a fresh to strong wind is likely to follow.

During tests the wind grew perceptibly stronger within 6 hours of a mackerel sky lowering and thickening 57 times out of 196; within 12 hours, 97 times out of 196; and within 24 hours, on 158 occasions out of 196.

One final, and important, cirrocumulus lore:

Increasing cirrocumulus in the sky is a sign of weather deterioration, but when it is seen to be decreasing there will be an improvement.

Reliability rating: very good.

CIRROSTRATUS (Cs)

Cirrostratus – the high-level milky-yellow sheet of mist which casts a thin veil across the sun or moon – when seen after cirrus helps confirm the 95 per cent probability of rain and increased wind sometime over the next forty-eight hours. Even without a fore-warning appearance of cirrus there are some rules of thumb worth applying when Cs cloud is partnered by a fall in barometric pressure.

With a veering wind an increase in cloud cover and a fifty-fifty chance of rain should be expected. With a backing or westerly wind it is 95 per cent certain to become wet and windy. With a southerly, easterly or northerly wind it will become cloudier and showery.

ALTOCUMULUS (Ac)

If clouds maintained their allotted stations in life the whole business of identification would be that much easier. Unfortunately, they don't. All of which wouldn't matter greatly to the weather watcher if it were not so difficult for dunderheads like me to judge heights in space and so distinguish, for instance, a medium-level cloud from one that is coasting around a few thousand feet higher up in the air. Thus, normal low-level stratus is sometimes difficult, and occasionally virtually impossible, to differentiate from altostratus which occupies the next deck up, while altocumulus can easily be confused with its higher flying cirrocumulus lookalike.

There is, in actual fact, a visible difference between Ac and Cc. Cumulo-form clouds in their guise as

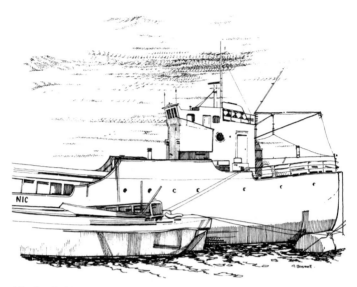

Mackerel skies – those tiny dots of cirrocumulus – are nothing to worry about, unless they start to thicken and gradually fall in altitude

cirrocumulus at the very peak of their profession appear as no more than a cluster of very white dots; they have no shadow and virtually no discernible shape. The much lowlier altocumulus, on the other hand, can, as already mentioned, be identified by the obvious light and shade of individual cloudlets. But don't worry about it overmuch because both formations provide similar sorts of forecasts, pretty well summed up by:

> *Mackerel scales,*
> *Furl your sails,*

and,

> *Mackerel sky*
> *Rain is nigh.*

Reliability rating for both: virtually the same as for cirrocumulus. Mark you, just the way it was with Cc, a mere trace of an altocumulus sky is not enough to predict the likelihood of rain and wind. And the barometer has to be falling, too. There has to be a fairly thick gathering of medium-level globular elements in order to forecast the possibility of weather deterioration; think, initially, in terms of about one-eighth of the sky filling and swelling with Ac mackerel scales. Then keep a constant eye on the barometer; if it so much as twitches towards the lower ends of the scale it is always wise to anticipate stronger winds.

On the other hand, if the barometer remains rigidly steady, or even rises, then forget any forebodings of gloom and doom. Look forward, instead, to an entirely more optimistic weather picture of sun, blue skies and gentle winds – unless the wind backs and increasing cloud and rain is very likely. Only when Ac and a falling barometer go hand in hand are heavy rain and winds on the way.

If altocumulus appeared in no other form, there would be few problems presented by this cloud formation. Unfortunately, it crops up within the middle-height sky regions in all sorts of guises, such as:

Lens-shaped clouds
The official term for this formation is *altocumulus lenticularis*, meaning that it is a middle-height cumulus cloud shaped like a lens. Visualise a convex lens viewed from the side, and you'll have the picture. Or if that's not graphic enough, think of it as the shape of a Churchillian cigar hanging in the middle sky.

Our forefathers, it seems, must have had more imagination than us because they called the same cloud the 'ark' or 'Noah's ark':

> *When the ark is out,*
> *Rain is about.*

Lens clouds provide a number of weather alternatives, depending on the direction of the wind

Others, no doubt the ones who farmed the sea from little boats, reckoned that it looked more like a fish:

> *The hake-shaped cloud indicates rain.*

Reliability rating: depends on several factors, so I have drawn up my own set of rules according to the results from a long series of observations. To qualify properly there has to be more than just a single cloud; two or three is better, a cluster of the little perishers is ideal.

> *Lens clouds with a veering wind presage fine weather.*
>
> *Lens clouds with a backing wind provide a fifty–fifty chance of rain.*
>
> *Lens clouds towards the east when a westerly wind is blowing promise fine weather.*

Lens clouds in the west with a westerly wind foretell an overcast sky and likelihood of rain.

Lens clouds with a southerly wind bring rain showers. With an easterly wind the weather will stay dry – as it will with a northerly wind except for people living in the vicinity of north-facing coasts.

Reliability ratings: very good for all the above.

Fleecy altocumulus

Massed layers of middle-height cumulus (altocumulus) build up ahead of calm weather.

Reliability rating: excellent. Recognition factor: a scramble of middle-height cumulus clouds which do not possess the well-regulated mackerel-scale patterns of traditional altocumulus skies.

This formation, despite the seemingly threatening appearance of any sky associated with increasing cloud cover and a generally gloomy appearance, retains all the hallmarks of fair-weather cumulus: cushiony, cotton-wool clouds which, although congregated into a despondent looking mass, lack the necessary depth for showers or any other bad-weather characteristics although they can, from time to time, accompany fairly high winds. Some rules of thumb:

1 An altocumulus fleecy layer is an omen of settled weather.
2 With a backing wind the cloud cover will increase, but there is still little chance of rain.
3 A veering wind with altocumulus fleeces will generally change to a southerly direction.

Ragged, jagged altocumulus

Long parallel bands of cumulus clouds which look like castle ramparts precede a storm.

Reliability rating: excellent, especially when the barometer is low (ie 1010mb or less) and falling. Recognition factors: this cloud formation is what the met men know as *altocumulus castellanus*, and that is precisely what it is – fairly well regimented lines of cumulus with flattish bases but ragged, tufted tops similar to irregular castellations on castle ruins. It appears in the middle-sky level and frequently carries with it outriders which old people used to liken to a 'flock of unkempt sheep' and our nowadays met men know as 'floccus'.

If this description has still not made the whole thing clear, try visualising a long line of flat pancake-like clouds which have been whisked into a froth of whipped cream and then flopped down onto a flat surface.

With a veering wind there is a 65 per cent chance of Ac *castellanus* bringing violent showers and some over-energetic wind squalls. With a backing wind you can be sure that thundery outbreaks are nearby six times out of ten in average temperatures, but eight times out of ten whenever the weather is warmer than normal.

There are a number of wind/*castellanus* permutations worth noting:

1 A fifty-fifty chance of heavy showers with a westerly wind.
2 Thunderstorms with a southerly wind – especially in the afternoon or evening.
3 Sunny periods and intermittent showers with an easterly or northerly wind.
4 Invariably, Ac *castellanus* bring winds, which often gust as strong as Force 7.

Chaotic altocumulus

> *Chaos in the sky,*
> *Chaos on the earth.*

Reliability rating: excellent, especially if the barometer is somewhere below the 1010mb mark and falling. The two factors go together: a chaotic jumble of cloud in the sky, chaotic weather down below.

This provides the beautiful but menacing abstract portrayals of sky chaos beloved by artists in dramatic mood. Usually, it is seen as a swirling yet strangely stagnant jumble of twisting cotton-wool cloud elements which have climbed upwards from low-level cumulus mounds. The result is a scrambled mess of cloud and sky colour, with fragments of dark-blue sky often still visible between the black, grey and white confusion of writhing cloud.

It is a portent of heavy rain, violent winds and outbreaks of thunder. Sometimes, though, a veering wind will help brush away the threat of thunder, and even rain at times, but you can be sure that huge wind gusts will still be plummeting earthwards.

Chapter Eight

HUMOROUS CUMULUS AND STRATUS SHROUDS

Cumuloform clouds come basically in three varieties, with characteristic similarities but entirely different weather-making abilities. First there is the darling of picnickers, the epitome of summer days – those miniature wodges or flecks of cotton wool which float good-naturedly beneath sunny skies. They appear, primarily, as individual brilliant-white puff-balls or massed into a plumped-up pillow of cloud with flattish base and subdued, puffy tops. Entirely devoid of malice, these are the very nicest form of cumulus, the better class of cloud entirely, much given to sharing dry and settled weather. They can be simply distinguished from their more malicious-minded brethren by a lack of vertical development which results in a base-to-lid distance measuring less than that from base to earth. Put another way, the thickness of fair-weather cumulus is seldom extraordinary and rarely more than 1,500ft (457m) from top to bottom.

The second, less lovable, type is shower cumulus. It looks a lot nicer than it actually is – a billowing, cauliflower-headed formation swollen to such a vertical extent that sunshine-flecked towers and rocky pinnacles sprout from the peaks. Heavy showers are to be expected, with gusty surface winds.

Thirdly, there is the ominous evil-black cumulonimbus (Cb) – the brooding, blackening (*nimbus*, in fact, means 'black') thunderheaded brother of baby cumulus. A veritable mountain of dense cloud which often measures as much as 45,000ft (14km) from base to top, its upper

Scurrying and bouncing towards the coast in our weary Morris car

regions are sometimes smooth, sometimes fibrous and sometimes with a characteristic top flattened into a projecting plume of upper-sky cirrus which looks very much like the tip of a blacksmith's anvil.

CUMULUS (Cu)

Humorous cumulus,
Never gloomerous.

Reliability rating: excellent. Frankly, this is another adage which cannot be truly allocated a place in the annals of weather lores. My father used to chant it aloud – 'an exceeding poor thing, but mine own', he boasted – as we scurried and bounced within the confines of our weary Morris Eight towards the coast on mornings when blue skies and puffy fair-weather cumulus promised a day so fine that even Dad might eventually dare a big toe into the sea. As I understand it, the rhyme is a play on the Latin designation of fair-weather *cumulus humilus* clouds and a tortuous tongue-twist of the word 'gloomy'.

Whenever fair-weather cumulus predominates, the day or night will remain generally fine with no chance of rain except, just possibly, over hills. Winds will very probably be somewhere between Force 2 and 4 by day, and substantially less by night; there is always, however, a chance of much stronger wind gusts beneath the swelling bank of cumulus clouds which lack the necessary height to threaten showers.

The effect of sea breezes (see page 116) is likely to be felt as much as 10–15 miles (16–24km) out to sea (on very rare occasions even further) and a goodish distance inland. Visibility will rarely be less than several miles during the summer half of the year, although there is always the possibility of haze near the coast. The barometer will be steady or rise only slowly. Any fall at all in the presence of fair-weather cumulus indicates the probability of an approaching depression.

Wind effect on cumulus skies should be taken into account:

1 Cu and a veering wind: good, dry weather, becoming bright – unless it is that way already when it will almost certainly remain unchanged – with steady, decent winds.
2 Cu and a backing wind: becoming cloudier in a matter of hours, probably with a fall in the barometer and strengthening winds.

3 Cu and a westerly: dry, set fine.
4 Cu and a southerly: dry, sunny and warm.
5 Cu and an easterly: becoming cloudier with wind gusts and a threat of showers later.
6 Cu and a northerly: light showers possible, but generally fine in the occasional gaps between the clouds and a fresher wind.

Cumulus clouds carry their own winds with them.

Reliability rating: excellent. As individual cumulus clouds approach, whatever their shape and size, the wind gusts and veers in a predictable sequence. Then as the cloud passes away, the wind backs again and lulls. It is a set, orderly pattern of events which never alters whenever the sky is patchy blue with plenty of individual Cu scurrying around overhead and the mean wind strength is somewhere between Force 1 and 5. It is not easy to judge, it is not easy to put into practice, but wise sail-boat men can, and do, learn to make the most of wind changes beneath a cumulus sky.

It works like this. As the blue gap ahead of an individual Cu element approaches, a gust is imminent and will occur with as much as a 40 degrees clockwise veer on inland waters and about 20 degrees well out to sea. Approaching gusts can be spotted by wind ruffling the water to windward, where other craft will heel in the sudden squalls. After the gust-veer sequence the wind direction will remain constant for a matter of minutes until the pattern is reversed: the wind slowly backs and gradually falls as it returns to its normal mean wind direction.

The bigger the cloud, the longer each gust sequence will last and can be as strong as 20–30 knots. Observation at the time will indicate the actual sequence timing of cumulus formations. To a great extent it depends on where you are. In open waters not far off the coast, when the mean wind is blowing about Force 3–4, the gusts tend to arrive every two or three minutes. On enclosed waters well inland from the coastal region they come much more often, which frequently makes tacking in phase impossible. Well out to sea they arrive, on average, in ten-minute phases. A tactical tip for racing sailors may not be out of place in a book on weather lore; port tack in the lulls and starboard tack in the gusts; tack immediately in light and moderate winds when the jib lifts appreciably at the luff.

The gust pattern remains the same even for the biggest of fair-weather Cu formations, but it alters when they become potential shower makers. The wind gusts and backs ahead of a sprawling billow of shower and thunder clouds, and veers to a lull after they pass by.

Bawlies fly in the wind.

Reliability rating: excellent, in as much as bawlies tell you what you almost certainly already know: it's breezy! They are not much by way of weather tellers, little more than windy adornments.

East-coast fishermen have always called the torn-paper scraps of high-flying cumulus clouds, sometimes seen beneath big-brother Cu formations, 'bawlies'. They are just what they seem – tattered, ragged bits and pieces of a larger, slower moving bank of cloud to windward. Officially, bawlies are known as *fracto-cumulus*.

Ragged cumulus clouds in the morning, bring showers and wind later in the day.

Reliability rating: very good as a warning of what might possibly occur, but not worth counting on more than six times out of ten. The presence of ragged, jagged-edged Cu in the early morning indicates a possible deterioration towards early afternoon only if there is a general foreboding 'feel' about the day. There is, in fact, a 75 per cent chance that, when conditions at, say, nine or ten o'clock in the morning look at all questionable whatever the cloud, you may not like them at all after midday when winds could be fresh or even strong and the sea a distinctly unlovable lumpy mess.

This is far from an immutable lore of the sky – if, indeed, there is such a thing. But it does serve as an excellent reminder that the weather is always changing and that you should trust your instincts.

Cumulus clouds inland of the coast with clear skies over the sea are signs of a good sea-breeze day.

Reliability rating: excellent, indicating exactly what it says: a nice, steady sailing breeze off the sea by day followed by a land breeze at night (see Chapter 12 for additional information on sea and land breezes). It's the sort of day when you could regret not having left the garden patch for the freedom of the waves.

The day will stay dry and fine, with clear visibility at sea and a possible trace or two of haze further inland. Winds will be Force 2–3 by day blowing onshore, and Force 1–2 by night blowing off the land. The barometer will be steady or rise only slowly; any fast rise indicates a possible weather deterioration in twelve to fifteen hours, any fall at all indicates approaching poor weather.

Fair-weather cumulus presages fine nights.

Reliability rating: excellent. Sunny and bright skies during an afternoon populated with fair-weather cumulus clouds, are followed by a night ideal for coastal passages. Any fair-weather cumulus sky is unlikely to deteriorate in less than twenty hours.

There will be steady and gentle nocturnal winds off the land, a benign sea and good visibility. Be wary, though, of winds which fall completely calm at sunset; they produced fitful and irritating breezes close inshore during night-time test observations five times out of ten (check out additional information on sea breezes in chapter 12).

> *The deeper the cloud,*
> *The harder it showers.*

Reliability rating: excellent. First, a couple of rules of thumb to go with this adage: shallow cumulus clouds bring dry weather; deep cumulus clouds always carry rain showers with them.

Cumulus clouds indicate continuing dry weather, until they begin thickening appreciably and their base becomes darkened by showers approaching, usually from the west. Generally speaking, the deeper, denser and darker the cloud, the harder, more persistent, the resulting showers will be. There is a fairly thin dividing line between cumulus clouds which only threaten showers and cumulonimbus clouds which virtually guarantee them. The heads of shower cumulus are solid and rounded, much like the irregular tops of cauliflower florets. They lack the growth, spindly chimneys and rocky projections of cumulonimbus, which is a much darker grey and sometimes almost black.

Cumulus shower clouds bring rain 50 per cent of the time; cumulonimbus (Cb) brings showers which are heavy and prolonged 87 per cent of the time. Better results, as a matter of fact, were expected. Remember, though, that a shower falls over a relatively small area and may not, therefore, have reached my own observation locality. I estimate that in reality there is a good 99 per cent chance of someone, somewhere, getting drenched by a Cb cloud.

Forecast a strong possibility of heavy showers with a

Force 3–5 wind (gusting at times to Force 6 and even 8) when you see cumulus showerheads developing. When there is a mingling of different types of cloud with large Cu formations present, the wind-shifts will be particularly fierce when the upper and lower clouds move in the same direction.

The approach of cumulus clouds with spreading, sprawling tops signifies the end of a bad weather spell.

Reliability rating: excellent. When cumulus monsters begin to displace the medium-height altostratus or altocumulus formations of a cold front bad-weather depression (see chapter 13 for a blow-by-blow account of a passing depression) then it is time to look for a gradual improvement. Similarly, when Cu or Cb shower clouds become displaced by spreading, sprawling cauliflower formations, then a weather improvement can be expected.

First it will remain cool, showery and thundery, then become progressively better as the cumulus clouds lose their individual towering pinnacles to become a spreading, homogenous mass.

1 With a veering, westerly or southerly wind it will become drier, brighter and generally much finer.

2 If the wind is backing, however, look for a slow build-up of deepening cloud behind a period of patchy blue skies.

3 With an easterly or northerly wind you can expect a continuing session of on-off showers followed by dry but cloudy and dull conditions.

Cumulonimbus presages heavy showers and possibility of thunder.

Reliability factor: excellent. Remember that cumulonimbus clouds are large, solid heads growing out of cumulus

An anvil cloud presages showers for sure; just how much rain depends greatly on wind direction

banks and possibly developing into an anvil shape at the peak. The dark-grey to black base will usually be accompanied by relatively low surrounding cloud.

Cb clouds don't always turn to thunder. About 60 per cent of the time they roll menacingly towards you, possibly give a couple of thunder claps, and then pass away after leaving a heavy drenching behind. Four times out of ten, however, they develop into monstrous thunderstorms, usually forewarned by the presence of attendant dark and sombre lower cloud crammed beneath the Cb elements.

When Cb threatens, forecast fast-deteriorating conditions, bringing heavy showers and a strong chance of thunder. Visibility will be poor during showery periods, which will send enormous wind gusts of 30–40 knots. The gust/lull pattern will last eight minutes on average, and wind-shifts will be as much as 60 degrees from the mean wind direction (90 degrees is not unknown). The following is a possible Cb wind-gust sequence based on average test results:

1 Wind backs 45 degrees just ahead of a strong gust rated at about 25 knots which lasts for 2 minutes;
2 The wind perceptibly lulls for 3 minutes;
3 The wind gusts again for 2 minutes while it veers progressively towards the original wind direction.

There are a number of general weather permutations which it is as well to take into consideration, depending on whether the Cb formation has an anvil peak:

Cb with anvil

1 With veering wind: showers will eventually die out to leave sunny, dry periods.
2 With backing wind: heavy showers and thunder likely to continue for some time.
3 With westerly wind: heavy showers very probable over land, but less predictable over the sea. In any case, areas on a western-facing coast will frequently remain dry.

4 With southerly and easterly winds: heavy showers and thunder.

5 With northerly wind: heavy showers but less likelihood of thunder.

Cb without anvil

1 With veering or backing winds: heavy showers and thunder.

2 With westerly wind: violent squalls, thunder and showers, brighter later.

3 With southerly wind: thunder, showers and wind squalls.

4 With easterly wind: thunder, showers and violent squalls with massive wind-shifts.

5 With northerly wind: thunder, showers and violent squalls.

STRATUS

One final item on cloud lore and the subject may be considered exhausted, at least so far as my own observations are concerned. It relates to stratus – that more or less uniform layer of grey cloud which is just as dull as it sounds. Nearly everybody knows what stratus looks like – a sky-borne fog which shrouds the earth in a wrapping of heavy lead. Break it into bits and pieces and it appropriately becomes fractured stratus or, more properly, *fraco-stratus*.

Either as a plain featureless grey sheet or as a bundle of fracto-stratus, it signifies gloomy but dry weather. When it is even more dreary and rain-sodden than normal it is known as *nimbo-stratus*; break this into fragments and you have the 'scud' of sailormen. Observations of 717 skies which I considered grey enough to rate as *nimbo-stratus* resulted in rain within two hours on 587 occasions, ie 82 per cent or about eight times out of ten.

Chapter Nine

GRANDAD'S TOE

It is a proven fact that a great many organisms respond in some way or other to changes in humidity and atmospheric pressure. Animal lovers claim that their pets warn them as much as a whole day before a storm approaches – normally dreamy horses turn rogue, dogs and cats grow restless or may slink into a corner to sleep. The sailormen who once steered their stately sailing barges through the mudbanks of south-east England believed whole-heartedly in the ability of dogs to 'smell' the wind, and rarely failed to ship a canine crew before proceeding to sea. Farmers claim that cows turn perverse and unruly before a storm. Fishermen believe that fish bite better. Ants are known to shore up their tunnels against an approaching deluge. Even scientists, who find it difficult to give credence to anything smacking even remotely of the occult, now agree that animals are able to detect some weather changes using a mysterious inbuilt detection system. Apparently we are able to do it, too. Quite a lot of people claim to have a sixth sense about a brewing storm – particularly the aged, the allergic, the overweight and the hypersensitive. They 'feel it in their bones'.

Don't scoff, it may not be imagination. Scientists reckon that definite changes take place somewhere within our bodies when there is a surge or fall in atmospheric pressure. In a two-year study in the United States, arthritic patients were sealed in special climate chambers for periods of two to four weeks. Nothing untoward was reported until researchers simulated the approach of a storm by gradually dropping pressure and boosting humidity. The results were quite astonishing: eight out of ten patients reported stiffness and swelling in their joints, and some reported the symptoms only minutes after the pressure change had started to take place.

So don't laugh at your grandfather's big toe. Take the thing with you when you and your little ship are off into the bright-blue yonder. Take grandad as well, if you must.

Another thing. Don't put your crew's ability to be dafter than most down to natural stupidity. It might be the weather. Many medical men sincerely believe that we become sillier or smarter according to the state of the day. In a voluminous tome, *Mainsprings of Civilization*, the late Dr Ellsworth Huntington reported that more than one-third of the religious riots which took place in India between 1919 and 1941 occurred during the hottest, stickiest Punjab months of April and August. In the western world, people investigated in eight cities withdrew more books of a serious-minded nature from their local libraries in winter and early spring than at other times of the year.

In another work – this time by E. O. Dexter – weather emerged as the probable reason for population explosions and slumps. And those who don't have the energy or inclination to make love, go round bashing up other people. After studying some 40,000 assault and battery arrests in New York City, Dexter found that the rate of increase in such incidents exactly paralleled the rise in temperature: in January the figures for arrest were low, in July they hit a peak. Dexter concluded that temperature, more than any other condition, 'affects the emotional states which are conducive to fighting'.

Rubbish? Possibly, but there does appear to be a clear relationship between tempers and temperature, just as winds seem to have a profound effect on our behaviour patterns. In southern France, the *vent du Midi*, a particularly warm and moist wind, is commonly blamed for Frenchmen punching up other Frenchmen and for an annual epidemic of headaches, rheumatic pains, epileptic fits, asthma attacks and some types of infant illness. The cyclonic storms that regularly plough through the mid-western states of the USA were described by Dr Clarence A. Mills in *Climate Makes the Man*, as 'leaving behind them a trail of human wreckage – cases of acute appendicitis, respiratory attacks of all kinds, and suicides'.

Some investigators are convinced that the peoples of Northern Europe work better, and get more done than those living on the hotter side of the tropical belt, because they never suffer the debilitation caused by the oppressive warmth of high summer. But we who live beneath the all too often gloomy skies of Britain, are far from free of weather-swept woes. A nameless east wind that still blows over London in November and March was blamed in the eighteenth century for 'black melancholy spreading over the nation'. According to the French writer Voltaire, dozens of dispirited Londoners hanged themselves over the fighting bodies of dogs and cats while all around 'people grew grim and desperate'. There was even an east wind blowing when Charles I was beheaded and James II deposed.

Even your marriage – supposing you have one – is not safe from the weather! According to Dr Mills, as a storm front approaches we are unaccountably bothered by a 'feeling of futility, an inability to reach the usual mental efficiency or to accomplish difficult tasks. Such weather provides the most perfect background for marital outbursts'.

Chapter Ten

NIGHT OWLERS

The ancients believed that

> *The screeching owl indicates cold or storm,*

which would provide a more or less cut-and-dried guide to night-time weather. Unfortunately there is an equally old adage which maintains

> *If owls hoot at night expect fair weather*

and another which says

> *In England, the owl's calling heralds hailstones.*

Yet again,

> *The whooping of an owl was thought once to betoken a change of weather from fair to wet, or wet to fair. But the owl when it hoots clearly and freely, generally shows fair weather, especially in winter.*

Reliability rating: all nil. Not surprisingly they all turned out a resounding flop during tests and merely provided confirmation, if any was needed, that owls ignore the weather and hoot, shriek or whoop because that's the way they hunt or, at breeding time, let intruders know they don't like interruptions.

After a long and arduous search for accurate weather

All old weather lore sayings involving owls turned out to be surprising and resounding flops

lores relating to creatures of the night I am reluctantly drawn to the conclusion that yesterday's people knew no more about the whole business than we do, but for one splendid exception:

> *When bats appear very early in the evening and in great numbers after the sun has set expect fair weather.*

Reliability rating: very good – an eight out of ten winner. The favourite food of the Common Bat is the insects which only venture abroad in excessive numbers when the weather is settled. Ergo, when bats appear from their daytime slumbers unusually early, or when a great many of them are airborne after dark, it is a pretty safe bet that they are onto a real feast and fine weather is, therefore, indicated. By and large, though, it is far from easy to predict weather changes after sunset. One of the banes of a night sailor is that bad weather can sidle in without anyone noticing.

It would be very nice to pretend that a handful of after-dark weather lores will help solve the problem, after all there are enough eerie alarms to disturb the peace and tranquility of a night passage as it is. All that velvet blackness, for one thing, with weird monsters rising and falling on the sea's swoop, and the neck-prickling 'glop, glop' of invisible beasts as they flick a tail of hissing surf somewhere off the starboard quarter. There are the real difficulties, too. The risk of a man slipping overboard is always greater at night-time than during the day; and the problems of coastal identification, judging a boat's speed, estimating wind strengths and predicting the weather, are all that much harder at night. Added to the fact that man is not naturally a nocturnal animal, these factors are often enough to keep the newcomer to boating firmly chained to a harbour mooring.

But he or she won't stay there for ever. Sooner or later, the initial fears of the unknown will be cast aside as a tremulous skipper points his bow towards the sea at the fall of darkness. Or, much more likely, he will be forced to stay at sea as the light fades because a tide has been lost or the wind has failed. So, in order to ease that plunge into the unknown, let's look at the weather problem.

First, once your eyes have become accustomed to the dark – even during the blackest hours – it is surprising just how much of the sky's features can be seen clearly. Cloud shapes and their related weather lores can be just as much help at night as during the day. Secondly, the night sailor will certainly have seen the sun go down in the evening and be awake when it rises next morning, and so be able to make the most of the associated important sky signs.

Thirdly, never overlook the fact that the magic sensory system of the barometer is always on watch, day and night. Always, always keep a weather-eye on the glass, but perhaps never more so than at night. Fourthly, never miss shipping forecasts if you can possibly help it; they may be somewhat out-of-date by the time they come over the air waves, may not be 100 per cent reliable, may only rarely be fully appropriate to your particular sailing locality – but they do, at the very least, provide a clue to the general weather picture which a knowledge of weather lores can help update and apply to local areas.

Lastly, there are some old lores which are exclusive to the night, although it does seem that grandfather and his lady spent most nights safely tucked into bed and so never got round to coining a lot to do with after-dark adages.

FULL MOON

A full moon, rising clear, foretells fair weather.

Reliability rating: excellent. My weather logs indicate that a clear full moon is invariably accompanied by perfect night-time weather.

RED MOON

If the full moon rises red, expect wind. When it rises red and appears larger than normal expect rain and wind within twelve hours.

Reliability rating: very good; correct on test eight times out of ten, but the moon has to be distinctly red (see following adage). This saying, in actual fact, relates to the weather which will occur next day, rather than during the coming night. For the hours of darkness until probably just before dawn the weather will, 86 per cent of the time, remain much like it was during the preceding day. Naturally, if the weather was noticeably deteriorating just before sunset, your night-time sail could well be a hairy one.

RED-BROWN MOON

*If the moon appears a reddish-brown through the haze,
the weather will stay fair.*

Reliability rating: excellent; correct on test nine times out of ten and fully applicable to the weather during the coming night.Any moon, however, which can fairly be described as 'red' can be counted on to presage wind.

PALE MOON

*Pale moon,
Rain soon.*

Reliability rating: good; correct 67 per cent of the time on test. A pale moon hints of high humidity or thin cloud in the upper layers of air and so the chance of rain subsequently is fairly high.

MOON HALO

The moon with a circle brings water in her beak.

*The moon, governess of the floods,
Pale in anger washes the air,
When round the moon she wears a brough [halo]
The weather will be cold and rough.*

Reliability rating: very good, scoring eight out of ten. A halo round the moon, as around the sun, indicates that humidity is increasing, a depression could be on the way, and that rain with stronger winds is likely by early morning. Once again, these two adages are not really applicable to conditions during the night. During tests involving moon haloes, rain occurred within six hours of sunset on only 2 occasions out of 10, and 4 times out of 10 within twelve hours. The halo scored 8 out of 10, though, for rain within thirty-six hours. In all instances the setting sun had also indicated the likelihood of rain.

MOCK MOONS

If two or three moons appear at a time it presages great wind and rain and unseasonable weather for a long time to come.

Reliability rating: excellent in parts, poor in others. The 'two or three moons' refer to mock moons which foretell on average an 80 per cent chance of rain and fresh winds within thirteen hours. Only on 3 out of 21 sightings (in my experience mock moons are a far from common occurrence) did the deteriorating weather last longer than what I would call 'a long time to come'.

CLEAR MOON

Clear moon,
Frost soon.

Reliability rating: very good; correct 8 times out of 10. This one is, I suppose, not much use to most sailors who generally set sail only in the summer months. Useful, though, for those on the beach who turn gardeners in winter when a cloudless night is almost certain to be followed by a frosty morning.

STARLIT NIGHT

When the sky seems overfull of stars expect new winds and anticipate rain.

99

Reliability rating: excellent, scoring 83 per cent rights in tests for forecasting a strengthening wind during the night and a fifty-fifty chance of rain.

FLICKERING STARS

When the stars flicker in a dark sky, rain or snow follows soon.

Reliability rating: very good; in 78 per cent of tests rain fell before dawn. The maxim refers to star flicker rather than twinkle; flickering stars are seen when the sky becomes overcast with cloud, and rain within about six hours is likely. Twinkling stars are nearly always the result of a clear, cold airstream when the wind is usually blowing from north-west to north-east. Rain is not indicated by excessive twinkling, despite a number of old lores which maintain that it is.

FADING STARS

When stars disappear,
Then rain and wind is near.

Reliability rating: excellent, providing you accept that the word 'near' refers to the rain being somewhere between two and four hours away and fresher winds about four or six hours off.

And that's about it for night-time weather lores; a poor showing considering that originally something like eighty-five after-dark sayings were put to the test. Personally, I still pin most of my faith upon the reliability of sunset sky-signs and identifying clouds in the night sky, rather than on the smattering of specialised night-time lores.

Chapter Eleven

CAPRICIOUS WINDS

As it happens we still don't know very much more about the winds than our forefathers did, despite all the inquisitive probes which modern man has thrust at the skies. And so, they remain among the most mysterious elements of our fickle weather. Most of Britain's ever-changing ever-capricious winds originate within a swirling vortex of atmospheric instability somewhere above the Atlantic Ocean. The result is a permanent state of scrambled confusion as vast airborne eddies form into swirling masses which eventually move, on a seeming whim of pace and direction, towards the British Isles. It is largely because that pace and direction is virtually unpredictable, that our official met men so often get their forecasts wrong.

The wind systems surge and subside, are born and die, become part of the cyclones and anticyclones beloved of the meteorologist. The rest of us, who are not so great, prefer to call them lows and highs.

It seems to me that we might just as readily call a budgie an eagle as refer to our piddling depressions as cyclones, for we in these fortunate isles are only rarely visited by the tropical storms which the very name 'cyclone' implies. Nor, for that matter, do we suffer much by way of regional, persistent winds such as the chinook of the Rockies, the föhn of the Alps, the zonda of the Andes, or the mistral which blows south from Burgundy during spring and autumn. 'An impetuous wind', wrote the Greek geographer Strabo of the mistral in the first century AD, 'which displaces rocks, hurls men from their chariots, crushes their limbs and strips them of their clothes and arms'.

Mind you, we stoic Brits have been known to do our share of stiff upper-lipping when it comes to weather hardships. Just imagine the phlegm of bravado which was displayed when a tornado left a trail of broken slates and chimney pots from South Devon to Cheshire on 27 October 1913. And how 'good in a crisis' the good people of Cambridge must have been when, in 1885, a storm of equal fury wreaked havoc amidst Sunday slumbers, uprooting trees and stripping roofs clean off the houses before disappearing towards the North Sea.

But since anything like the full-blooded, raging tempests of the tropics seldom reach the British Isles, I shall continue to call the met man's cyclones either depressions or lows and refer to their mirror-image anticyclones as highs.

In the simplest of terms, a depression brings with it bad weather implying cloudy skies, wind squalls, rain and snow storms. Summer highs are expected to carry good weather in their tracks, although they are not to be trusted for, within their isobarometric web, lies the danger of thunderstorms, fogs and other weather beasties.

> *A very steep high, summer or winter, can produce strong winds around its outer edges.*
>
> *A winter high not infrequently brings with it dense cloud layers, winds and rains.*
>
> *In the early part of the year, well into the spring, a high can carry bitterly cold winds and grey murk — particularly when it settles to the north of Britain to whisk Arctic airs upon us.*

Reliability: at least 90 per cent. The above sayings are the result of accurate observations, but although highs do not invariably promise perfect, near-cloudless skies, that is what they bring nine times out of ten in a normal British summer. High-pressure systems with their associated ridges, as opposed to lows and troughs, can generally be looked upon as the good summer fairies of the weather world. They frequently remain stationary somewhere over or near the British Isles, bringing settled spells of fine hot weather in summer and perhaps a little haze.

The small, steep highs of the dogdays – weather breeders as the old-timers called them – occasionally squeeze themselves between a series of bad-weather lows and so produce a golden opportunity to make a fast passage home before the next low arrives. And the lows which follow these temporary breaks are often massive ones. By and large, highs are pleasant enough dullards. They dawdle about the heavens a good deal more than depressions and quite often last for days, sometimes weeks, on end. Lows, on the other hand, are a good deal more active, nipping about above Britain at a furious pace before dissipating in an average of five days. They cram a lot into a short time, bringing a lot of cloud, sunny intervals, huge bursts of wind, lashing rains and just about anything nasty you can think of. Lows are aggressive beasts with a militant tendency to turn yachts into cocktail shakers:

> *A nasty nature is the role of lows,*
> *Rainy days and windy blows.*

So what do we know about the winds each type of pressure system brings? Not a lot. We do know that the wind blows in an anticlockwise direction round a low-pressure centre while incling inwards slightly towards the heart of the depression. It blows clockwise round a high and spins, like a scrap of paper on a slowly revolving record, slightly outwards from the centre. By applying this knowledge to the charts printed in those daily

103

newspapers which bother with such things, it is possible for the amateur weather watcher to work out a rough and ready guide to probable wind directions. Alternatively, and more sensibly, you can rely on the met man's official direction prediction which can seldom be bettered.

I wish the same was true of Met Office wind-speed predictions. They are not to be relied upon. I'm not sure just why this is unless, as I suspect, it has to do with the problems of accurately plotting the path and approach speed of a high or low and therefore predicting just when and where such and such a wind speed will be experienced. They do not succeed much better than 50 per cent of the time. I have known too many warnings of huge winds which failed to arrive to any longer rely unthinkingly upon warnings of gales. Conversely, I have stayed at home too many times when forecasted calms turned to brisk, ideal sailing winds. I now prefer to use my own senses and knowledge of the old weather lores.

For some reason, the down-to-earth wind lores coined by our forefathers have been allowed to fall into almost total disuse. Grandfather may not have known all, or any, of the scientific facts about the wind which are now, supposedly, at our electronic finger tips; but he did have the good sense to rely on generations of observations and experience to help keep him safe at sea. These wind lores deserve revival. One word to the wise, however; none of them should be regarded as dogma. They should be regarded as pertinent observations of general wind characteristics which, together with other weather lores, provide a broad and often accurate guide to the meteorological uncertainties caused by our unsettled climate.

The wind blows in plervets.

It does not take even the rawest of sailing recruits overlong to discover that there is no such thing as a constant, reliable wind. It never blows steadily, whether it be a winter's storm or a mild summer breeze, but always in what the old windmillers used to call 'plervets'. Met men may accurately forecast a north-westerly blowing Force 3, but this should never be considered anything more than a guide to mean wind speed and direction which, during a single day's sail, may shift as much as 180 degrees and swoop and fall by, perhaps, 20 knots. Any wind has a high and low gust-range with a speed that fluctuates within a few knots in as many seconds. The same is true of direction which is even more sensitive and often ranges over 60 degrees in just one second.

It is instructive to watch a wind generator. The vane is forever seeking this way and that, constantly swinging through about 10 degrees (and sometimes as much as 90 degrees) as it follows the wind's path, while the speed of the propeller surges and slows as the wind rises and falls. Just ten minutes spent watching such a device should make any sailor aware of the need for constant adjustment and readjustment of the set of a boat's sails.

Gusts are basically wind flurries which plummet to the surface from aloft. The biggest are usually associated with the passage of a cold front which marks the progression of a depression. In the British Isles they occur most frequently after the wind has veered by some 20 or 30 degrees to blow from a south-westerly or westerly wind direction.

All gusts are strongest when (a) sailing on landlocked waters; (b) sailing in the morning rather than the afternoon; (c) heaped cumulus and cumulonimbus clouds are about (the bigger the heaped clouds, the more gusty the wind, see pages 83, 89); (d) the mean wind speed is around 20 knots (gusts are always weaker when wind strengths are above or below Force 5); (e) thunderstorms are approaching or overhead, bringing intense gusts of 30 to 50 knots.

The bigger the heaps of cumulus and cumulonimbus, the more gusty the wind — especially on landlocked waters

Gusts do occur during light airs but they are difficult for the sail-boat man to seek out and utilise to the best advantage. In gentle to fresh breezes of Force 3–5, they occur at something like 2 to 6 knots stronger than the mean wind speed. Apart from during the lightest of airs, gusts are weakest when (a) far out to sea, (b) layer clouds predominate and visibility is generally poor, (c) one is sailing at night, evening and dawn.

> *Wind speed over the open sea is often twice what it is over land.*

Neither this nor the previous saying can be considered weather-forecast lores. They are, rather, statements of fact. The latter adage is a useful one to bear in mind, especially when you are in a sheltered harbour trying to decide whether or not to put to sea.

How to tell whether the wind outside is too strong? The best, surest, way is to ask your local weather station for guidance. Telephone and ask them for the mean wind speed, direction and average speed of the gusts. But, remember, a lot of weather stations are based inland so that the wind speed you are given is likely to be less than that experienced at sea. The biggest difference between land and sea wind speeds occurs with light winds. When wind Forces of 1–3 are relayed by a weather station, sea strengths will very possibly be somewhere between Force 1 and 5 by day and 1 and 4 by night. The strongest forces quoted by a weather station should be stepped up by about one additional Beaufort factor (say an extra 6 knots) for probable sea strengths.

Failing a telephone call to the local weather station, the next best indicator is the anemometer on the clubhouse or on a yacht at anchor. Alternatively, get out of the way of buildings, cliffs and trees and look straight into the eye of the wind. Then, to be on the safe side, step up your estimate. Either way, do not be content with anything short of three to five minutes' observation to give you the roughest guide to mean wind speed and direction.

> *When the rain's before the wind,*
> *Topsail halliards you must mind,*
> *If the wind's before the rain,*
> *Soon you will make plain sail again.*

Reliability rating: good. The couplets – true forecasting adages – refer to the supposed fact that when rain falls ahead of a strengthening wind, something like gale force can be expected; when the wind comes first, it will soon die away or never attain anything worse than a freshish breeze. I expected better from the results of tests into this saying; after all it is regularly quoted by most relevant textbooks and must have been doing the rounds for a long, long time. In fact, the pair of couplets each scored a fairly measly six out of ten, so consider the chances of a high wind after rain no better than fifty-fifty. The same is true when wind precedes rain. The only time you can count on the saying proving accurate is during a deep depression (see Chapter 13).

> *Another storm a-brewing –*
> *I hear it sing i' the wind.*

Reliability rating: between seven and eight times out of ten; in fact tests produced a 75 per cent result, ie 112 rights out of 148 observations. An approaching deterioration in the weather is often signalled, when at anchor, by aeolian music moaning through the boat's rigging; but not invariably. During the tests there were thirty-six occasions when I fully expected the whine of an early morning wind through the shrouds to turn into a regular thumper later in the day; in actual fact on seven mornings it gradually fell right away and the other times failed to develop significantly. During 112 observations, however, the wind slowly built up to an estimated Force 6 or 7 with rain, usually when the sky was an indeterminate jumble of bits and pieces of grey cumulus scudding beneath a totally overcast, lowering sky.

> *The winds of daytime wrestle and fight,*
> *Longer and stronger than those of the night.*

Reliability rating: excellent. Almost invariably it is possible to forecast that the wind will fall away and often collapse entirely by evening, so long as the day is not totally overcast. The wind usually begins to subside after the maximum daytime temperature at around 2–3 pm. An hour or two after noon is the period when winds blow their strongest. The greatest fall of all is just after sunset:

> *The smaller and lighter winds generally rise in the morning and fall away at sunset.*

Winds after sunset pick up slightly with the night and often shift direction, although dramatic gusts are seldom experienced after dark. The wind falls again towards dawn. It is equally true, however, that

> *A strong daytime wind remains at night and into the following day.*

> *If the wind at sunrise drives the clouds away,*
> *Fair weather is the order of the day.*

Reliability rating: excellent, scoring nine out of ten. There doesn't seem to be any reason to expand on this one; I merely point out that clouds breaking up at sunrise indicated a dry day with nothing stronger than Force 5 winds on 84 per cent of test observations.

> *The tide brings with it a new wind.*

I refuse to give this one an accuracy rating. I steadfastly try not to be lured by the adage because common sense dictates that it is impossible for the winds to change with the tide, any more than it is possible, as another adage has it, for

> *The moon and the weather [to] change together.*

Having said all that, I must admit to sitting, time and again, at a lifeless helm beneath limp sails secretly convinced that a new wind sometimes springs to life with the change of tide. Faced with good, sound, scientific arguments such faith is ridiculous, I refuse to believe in the silly saying. Privately, I still reckon it worth an accuracy mark of at least one (maybe two or three) out of ten.

109

Chapter Twelve

BOREAS, NOTOS, APELIOTES AND ZEPHYROS

The character of the winds does not change: not since Aristotle, in the fourth century BC, named the north wind Boreas, the south wind Notos, the east wind Apeliotes and the west wind Zephyros before describing with amazing accuracy the weather likely to be brought by each; not since Bartholomaeus Anglicus, a thirteenth-century scholar, noted:

> *The Northe winde . . . purgeth and cleanseth raine, and driveth away clowdes and mistes, and bringeth in cleereness and faire wether; and againward, for the South winde is hot and moyste it doth the contrary deedes: for it maketh the aire thicke and troubly, & breedeth darknesse.*

Today the methods of linking wind and weather are more sophisticated. Forecasters want to know first what the barometer is doing and only then which way the wind is blowing. Their findings, although more detailed, bear out the observations of the ancients:

> *When the wind sets in from points between south and south-east and the barometer falls steadily, a storm is approaching from the west or north-west, and its centre will pass near or north of the observer within 12 to 24 hours, with the wind shifting to north-west by way of south and south-west.*

Reliability rating: excellent, scoring better than 90 per cent accuracy marks out of eighty-five tests conducted in the British Isles. It's important to stress just where the tests were carried out because the above ruling comes from the United States Weather Bureau which issues a concise listing of wind, barometer and weather trends for regions all over the USA. The Meteorological Office does not supply any comparative listing; at least I have been unable to obtain one despite successive applications. So, to help compensate for that failing, your attention is drawn to the following wind/barometer rules of thumb laid down by the United States; they proved at least 70 per cent reliable in tests conducted within waters around the United Kingdom and are therefore recommended.

Wind SW to NW
Barometer 1020mb to 1023mb, steady: forecast fair weather with little temperature change for 1 or 2 days.
Barometer 1020mb to 1023mb, rising fast: forecast fair weather followed by rain within 2 days.
Barometer 1023mb or above, steady: forecast set fair with little temperature change.
Barometer 1023mb or above, falling slowly: forecast fair weather for 2 days, slowly rising temperature.

Wind S to SE
Barometer 1020mb to 1023mb, falling slowly: forecast rain within 24 hours.
Barometer 1020mb to 1023mb, falling fast: forecast steadily increasing wind, rain in 12 to 24 hours.

Wind SE to NE
Barometer 1020mb to 1023mb, falling slowly: forecast rain in 12 to 18 hours.
Barometer 1020mb to 1023mb, falling fast: forecast rising wind, rain within 12 hours.

111

Barometer 1016mb or below, falling slowly: forecast steady rain for one or two days.
Barometer 1016mb or below, falling fast: forecast rain and high wind, clearing within 26 hours.

Wind E to NE
Barometer 1020mb or above, falling slowly: forecast winds, rain not immediately likely in summer; rain within 24 hours in winter.
Barometer 1020mb or above, falling fast: forecast rain probable in summer within 24 hours; rain or snow and high winds in winter.

Wind E to N
Barometer 1016mb or below, falling fast: forecast severe gale, heavy rain.

Wind S to E
Barometer 1016mb or below, falling fast: forecast severe storm imminent, clearing within 24 hours.

Wind veering W
Barometer 1016mb or below, rising fast: forecast improving conditions.

Compared with such concise guides to the wind and weather as these, many of the old weather lores, sadly, do not stand up to detailed examination. There are one or two notable exceptions, all of which help to supplement the wind/barometer guidelines contained in the above.

NORTHERLY WIND

A north wind and falling barometer heralds cold rains in summer and severe frosts in winter.

When the wind is north or north-north-west during a

'The Northe wind purgeth and cleanseth raine; and againward, the South winde doth the contrary deedes'

wintry spell of cold weather, a sudden rise in the barometer denotes the approach of rain and a southerly wind.

EASTERLY WIND

With an east wind and a steadily falling barometer, the wind will soon go round to the south – unless a heavy fall of snow or rain follows immediately after.

SOUTHERLY WIND

South-east winds accompanied by a falling barometer, indicate a probable future wind veer to south or south-west and the possibility of thunderstorms in summer.

Winds from the south-east, accompanied by a falling barometer and rain, quite often turn into gale force; but they seldom last long.

When high winds from the south-west, south-south-west or west-south-west are accompanied by a falling barometer, a storm is probable. If the fall be rapid, the wind will be violent although short lived. If it be slow, the wind, while less violent, will be longer lasting.

A south wind and falling barometer are invariably followed by rain.

A rising barometer with a southerly wind is usually followed by fine weather – dry and warm in summer, dry with moderate frosts in winter.

A freshening southerly wind which backs to the south-east and is accompanied by a falling barometer foretells a probable rapid veer to south-west and later to west, when it may well turn to gale force.

WESTERLY WIND

When the wind is due west and the glass falls fast and sure, then a violent storm may be expected from the north-west or north.

Winds from a western quarter which veer towards north with a rising barometer are a sure indication that fair weather is on the way. But a westerly that backs towards the south-west with a falling barometer is a sign that bad weather is not far away.

> *Winter winds blowing strongly from the west together*
> *with a high and steady barometer, invariably bring*
> *high temperatures and very little rain.*

Some of the above adages smack of the absolute, predicting or implying an 'invariable' weather change. Don't unthinkingly pin your faith on any promised weather condition. Count upon them, as I do, proving right most of the time; but always be on the alert for the unexpected.

The above wind/barometer tips are supplemented by the information in Chapter 14. Meanwhile, the lores on backing/veering winds can be expanded and the captivating mystery of sea and land breezes examined.

BACKING/VEERING WINDS

> *A veering wind, fine weather,*
> *A backing wind, foul.*

Reliability rating: nearly very good, scoring an accuracy mark of 76 per cent in tests. As a general rule, when the wind turns against the sun (when it backs from, say, west to south) beneath a cold grey or dirty-yellow sky, it is attended by a falling barometer and the weather is very likely to deteriorate. When it swings on a parallel course to the sun (veers, say, from west to north) and the barometer rises, there is an excellent chance of fine weather.

The wind in front of a depression often backs first:

> *When the wind backs and the glass falls,*
> *Then be on your guard 'gainst gales and squalls.*

Reliability rating: goodish. When a strong wind backs, rain and violent winds are pretty sure to follow; a depression is almost certainly on the way. There are occasions, though, when the backing-veering rule can be turned topsy-turvy.

Nearly always a weather change for the worse follows whenever the wind backs decidedly from anywhere between north and west-south-west. But a wind which backs from any other quarter, unless there is a definite and perceptible fall in the barometer, should not be taken automatically as warning of a strengthening wind.

In fine weather the wind goes round with the sun.

Reliability rating: excellent. It is a reminder that a veering wind very often occurs when the day is set fine, and that the change indicates nothing of particular significance.

SEA AND LAND BREEZES

The lore covering sea breezes is a beguiling one.

Sea breezes blow towards the land during the day to be replaced by an offshore land breeze at night.

Reliability rating: excellent – in theory. During daylight hours the land warms up faster than the sea, supposedly sucking an onshore breeze towards the coast and so filling the vacuum left by strong thermal currents as they soar upwards from the land. After nightfall the effect is reversed, supplying coastal waters with a cup o' nocturnal breezes from the land until they lull and calm before changing again at dawn.

That's the theory – as neat a package of seemingly inevitable winds as any sailor could wish for. A pity, then, that the diurnal and nocturnal winds are nowhere so accommodating in practice. In thirty years of sailing around various bits and pieces of the British coastline, sea breezes have let me down as many times as they have served. So beware; do not be lured by the promise of regular day and night breezes from sea and land. Hope they will arrive; by all means, expect them; but never count on them until, that is, you head south from British waters and onwards into sub-tropical coastal regions where the onshore breeze and its nocturnal partner occur with almost clockwork regularity.

My logs show that the chance of getting a diurnal sea breeze on waters around the British Isles is no better than fifty-fifty – certainly far less than many of the sailing books and meteorological guides for mariners imply. The probability of having a noctural land breeze after dusk is fractionally, although not much, better.

It is useful to know just if a diurnal sea breeze or a nocturnal land breeze is going to blow. The following should help:

1 Sea breezes in the northern hemisphere are seasonal, so don't bother to look for them outside the warmer months of late spring, summer and early autumn.

2 They normally begin breezing in towards land after a lull in the wind just after dawn. If they haven't arrived by mid-morning, they are not going to turn up at all. They rise in strength to a peak by about 2 o'clock in the afternoon. By seven in the evening – or, at the latest, 10 o'clock – they will have died away to leave a calm before a new wind develops offshore at about the time when English publicans are thinking about calling 'Time, gentlemen, please!'

3 If a sea breeze continues onshore after dusk it is usually due to a change in barometric pressure, and generally forecasts the onset of deteriorating weather.

4 The nocturnal breeze will be at its strongest just after midnight and will die away sometime around, or just after, dawn.

117

5 The presence of cumulus clouds which extend 10 miles (16km) or so seawards, and something just less than that distance inland, boosts the chances of a sea breeze occurring. Ideal conditions include a day with plenty of blue sky and a regular parade of cumulus clouds.

6 The coasts which produce the most reliable sea breezes are those which face either east or south. Best of all are the same coasts backed by a range of low hills.

7 Sea breezes will not occur if (a) offshore winds at 9 or 10 o'clock in the morning are Force 3 or stronger; (b) the sky is overcast with low-lying cloud.

8 If the wind direction at about 9 o'clock in the morning is already more or less blowing off the sea, the effect of sea breezes will be to increase the wind's strength.

9 Early morning winds on typical sea-breeze days often double in strength by afternoon.

10 Even on sunny, perfect-cumulus days, sea breezes seldom reach much more than 10 miles (16km) or so out to sea.

11 Expect big and sudden wind-shifts when, instead of an onshore sea breeze, the early morning wind in summer is blowing from the land to the sea.

12 Fog and haze produce coastal calms which eliminate the chances of an early morning sea breeze; but the latter can often still occur later in the day if the fog clears.

13 Thunderstorms during the forenoon can destroy sea breezes, although there is a good chance they will return as the thunder moves away.

It is always a goodish tip to remember that, when an offshore wind is blowing at around 9 o'clock in the morning and is no more than light or gentle, there will probably be a sky-borne clash between a potential sea breeze and the gradient wind. The result is known as a 'sea-breeze front'. These fronts form more or less parallel ranks along the coast and can produce enormous wind-shifts of 180 degrees.

On east-facing coasts expect sea-breeze fronts to spin the wind from west to south-east and strengthen during the day by as much as an extra 3 to 10 knots. On south-facing coasts, the normal effect is for the wind to change in a massive swoop from southerly to north-westerly during the morning and become south-south-westerly by the afternoon.

A sea-breeze front is nearly always marked by a dark, deep line of cumulus cloud advancing towards the land on a course more or less parallel to the coast. Gulls can often be observed soaring in gigantic spirals beneath the approaching cloudbase while, close to land, curious shell-shaped cat's-paws fret about the hulls of moored vessels.

Watch the approaching cloud bench for it carries with it a fairly predictable wind-shift pattern which eager racing men and wise cruising skippers would do well to utilise. Ten to fifteen minutes before the front forces the clouds directly overhead, the wind will fall to near calm before backing for five to ten minutes and then veering in a similar five-to-ten-minute phase. At the same time the wind strength will surge and fall in fits and starts, before finally settling to a steady shorewards-blowing breeze as the clouds which mark the front pass towards the land and leave behind clear, sunny skies. Occasionally, the wind-shifts accompanying the front are turned turtle into a reverse-sequence veer-then-back pattern – a fairly rare but irritating occurrence which produces fitful and entirely unpredictable shifts.

119

On most coasts, during the summer months, the wind blows to sea at night. In fact, such a nocturnal breeze is virtually guaranteed during late summer and early autumn, providing the gradient winds at the time of the normal evening lull is not blowing any stronger than 6 knots. If the wind at around sunset is anything stronger than a light breeze, it is likely to be as late as midnight before the noctural wind arrives. If the wind at dusk is already blowing offshore, bear in mind that the potential nocturnal land breeze may well help strengthen the wind during the night.

A tactical, common sense tip for moonlighters is that, if the prevailing wind overnight looks like being a fitful, sloppy one, always try to sail as near the shore as prudent by midnight in order to take advantage of any nocturnal land breezes there may be.

Finally, a few pointers to the perfect conditions for a night-time land breeze:

1 A flat coastline backed by hills.
2 A clear, or near clear, sky, normal visibility and absence of low cloud.
3 Any high cloud should not be increasing substantially.
4 A weak gradient wind, for nocturnal breezes rarely exceed 6 knots except, occasionally, near coasts which are backed by high ground. Here night-time land breezes can reach 10 to 15 knots.

Chapter Thirteen

A DEPRESSING SEQUENCE

It is often possible for the weather watcher to track and timetable, in quite dramatic fashion, a depression passing across the British Isles. A number of clues have already been provided within several weather lores, but it is instructive to consider the precise sequence of sky, wind and barometer indicators.

First, some bare-bone facts. The majority of well-developed British low-pressure systems approach from the Atlantic and follow an east-north-east track towards the north and west of Scotland. A typical classic depression carries with it two fronts – a warm one first and then a cold one – which advance at an average speed of 31mph (50km/h). But no two depressions are alike, otherwise they could be plotted by professional meteorologists with graphic simplicity. Clouds, winds, the ups and downs of air pressure and even the character of fronts themselves vary one from another.

Warm and cold fronts can be neatly separated, and thus marked on weather maps. Frequently, though, they merge, leaving no clear boundary between them and so become part of an occlusion or occluded front. Fortunately, however, the sequence of weather events preceding an occlusion varies only in minor details from that running ahead of warm and cold fronts and so, in practice, the amateur weather watcher can virtually ignore the difference.

Depressions may take a far different journey from the classic one already outlined. Some may pass up the

English Channel. Others, particularly dotty ones which are determined upon doing entirely their own thing, may break their north-easterly track to double back in a westerly direction. Some may ease their way towards us from the north of France. Nevertheless, the depression-spotting rules are basically unchanged, depending on whether or not the observer is to the north or south of a low-pressure centre and assuming that most lows approach Britain, as they do, from the western half of the compass.

A good many hours before the approach of a warm or an occluded front, high clouds will nearly always provide a precursory hint of a weather change for the worse. Cirrus clouds, fanning their way eastwards, provide warning of a low when its warm front is still something like 500 miles (800km) away. Whether or not cirrus foretells a low for sure depends on a number of factors (see Chapter 7 for more on cirrus portents and Chapter 14 for barometer behaviour). Applications of the prime cloud lore (see page 63) will help you decide if a depression is on the way.

By and large, if ceiling-high mares' tail cirrus thickens and spreads to become a thin sheet of featureless cirrostratus (maybe in association with patches of mackerel sky) and then lowers to a much gloomier, much more foreboding altostratus, a depression in the offing is pretty well guaranteed. If, more or less at the same time, the wind backs even slightly, the barometer falls and the day slowly turns to a watery wash of grey, almost certainly a nasty natured low pressure system is spreading its web of wind and rain towards you.

The type of weather brought by a depression depends on just how intent it is to drench and brisken up the residents of these islands. The following account of conditions characteristically associated with well-developed depressions approaching the British Isles from the west, provides the sequence of events which can be expected about eight times out of ten. The exceptions vary only in degree and should, therefore, be easily spotted once the typical pattern is fixed clearly in the mind.

DEPRESSION CLOUDS

Tufts of mackerel clouds and mares' tails spread into a milk-white wash across the sky, before lowering into gloomy layers well before the arrival of rain and wind.

Reliability rating: excellent. This is another of the many weather-cloud lores covering the approach of a depression (see also Chapter 7). Unusually, this saying includes mackerel clouds along with the more commonly accepted mares'-tails warnings. It helps serve as a reminder that cirrocumulus, and to some extent altocumulus, formations, are sometimes seen well ahead of a depression.

Normally, however, thickening cirrus comes first. Cirrostratus and/or altostratus always appears. The sky becomes lower and lower, gloomier and gloomier. It is just possible sometimes to be deceived into predicting an approaching depression by the appearance of fairly low stratus at around the middle of the day along with a westerly wind and a thick veil across the sun. Unless, however, the weather appears altogether grubbier and is accompanied by a falling barometer and probably a backing wind, the cloud is almost certain to break up and pass harmlessly away during the afternoon.

The first rains will fall once the cloud has lowered and thickened deep enough, on average some twelve to fourteen hours after the first cirrus sightings in the sky. It will be light at first, then heavier and more persistent as the warm front moves past above a messy sky consisting of lower-layer stratus jumbled with dark-grey bits and pieces of *nimbo-stratus.*

As the warm front lumbers past expect a glimpse of

As the warm front lumbers past expect a glimpse of lightening sky behind the trailing cloudbase; but beware, for there is a cold front trying to catch up

lightening sky just behind the trailing cloudbase. There will be brighter periods and showers while the air will feel distinctly muggy. Prospects will definitely appear cheerier, but beware, for behind every warm front there is a cold front doing its level best to catch up; beyond the distant horizon will be great dollops of puffy clouds, with blotchy grey faces, bunched in an ominous fast-approaching line. This is the cold front, and it doesn't mess about the way warm fronts do.

The coming deluge will be sudden and heavy. The wind will pick up and fill, from a north-westerly quarter if you are positioned well to the south of the depression. Neither the rain nor the wind will cease until the depression passes away, marked by lifting cloud which turns to medium-height altostratus or altocumulus, then to ponderous cauliflower cumulus or cumulonimbus lurking amidst patches of well-washed greeny-blue skies. Remember, the bigger the clouds, the bigger the weather-woes they carry:

rain, hail, thunder and vicious winds pack these mountainous beasts with a terrible punch. Slowly, though, the weather will improve.

It is worthwhile considering the probable time interval between the first sky sighting of cirrus turning to cirrostratus and the eventual arrival of a front. Generally speaking, when the change from cirrus to cirrostratus is rapid, rain is about six hours away on average. The wind, however, will increase a good while before that (although quite possibly, not of any significantly greater strength) and certainly long before the cloud droops to altostratus. If the cirrus to cirrostratus sequence is slow, taking perhaps most of the day, stronger winds and rains will probably be a day or two further behind. At the rate of travel of a typical low there is often a time span of about fifteen hours between the first sky warnings and the arrival of warm front rains. Higher winds occur much sooner – roughly about six hours after cirrus significantly thickens and lowers.

Rain is imminent as soon as altostratus obscures the sun completely, with ragged swelling bits and pieces of grey clouds approaching from windward beneath the main cloudbase. Typically, it takes an average of four hours or, less often, six, for the rain from an active front to pass away.

DEPRESSION BAROMETER

At sea with a low and falling glass,
Soundly sleeps a careless ass.

Reliability rating: excellent. The barometer invariably falls before the onslaught of a depression, slowly at first but faster as the front gets nearer. A fall of 8 millibars in three hours omens gale-force winds, 5 millibars in three hours indicates probable Force 6, 3 millibars in three hours indicates lesser winds – but strong gusts will still occur.

Long foretold, long past,
Short notice, soon past.

Reliability rating: excellent. A barometer which falls over a period of a day or so indicates that a large and long-lasting low-pressure system is on the way. A sudden drop, especially if it is only a small one, gives warning of a tiny though active little perisher which is likely to pass by in no time at all and prove much less violent than its more persistent bigger brother.

A warning, though: small troughs which are only just registered by the barometer often slip past professional forecasters because they appear on their weather charts as nothing more than barely discernible blips. It is not unknown for them to suddenly deepen and spread.

The barometer sequence accompanying a low is just as precise as cloud activity:

1 Pressure falls all the time a warm front is approaching before steadying temporarily or at least slowing significantly at its arrival.
2 Rate of fall will step up again once a warm front has passed.
3 Pressure will rise, perhaps quickly, as a cold front passes away; should it fail to rise after the passage of a cold front, the probable reason is the presence of bitty low-pressure troughs.

WIND

If the wind shifts against the sun,
Trust it not, for back t'will run.

Reliability rating: generally no better than quite good. But when a backing wind is accompanied by a low-pressure cloud and barometer sequence, the adage rates as excellent. As a rule of thumb, remember that the wind normally backs then veers ahead of a warm front.

The wind sequence associated with a low depends on whether the observer is located south or north of the centre. It's not hard to find out:

In the northern hemisphere when you stand with your back to the wind the low-pressure area will be lower on your left hand than your right. The reverse is true in the southern hemisphere.

Naturally, it is important to know that the wind you are experiencing is actually part of a depression. Observation of cloud activity and the barometer should already have given a hint or two. So will application of the prime cloud lore (see page 63) while an up-to-date shipping or general weather forecast should have put you on your guard.

Wind sequence for an observer south of the centre (the position most frequently experienced by sailors in the English Channel, the Thames Estuary and the east coast) of an approaching depression is as follows:

1 Wind increases by as much as two Beaufort factors as it backs to south-west, south-south-west, south, or even south-south-east. Occasionally, when the wind is already somewhere in a southerly quarter, the backing sequence fails to occur.
2 When the warm front is imminent the wind will veer, probably to south-west or west, and decrease slightly in strength.
3 The wind will remain fairly steady, blowing on average somewhere between Force 1 and 6, until the cold front is close enough to cause the wind to back slightly when it will surge

to, perhaps, Force 6 to 7 (sometimes Force 8) accompanied by swingeing squalls.

4 As the cold front passes away the wind will veer towards a northerly quarter, often becoming north-westerly.

5 Lifting cloud cover as the cold front passes away is quite often accompanied by erratic wind behaviour, backing and veering before and after squalls, decreasing and increasing suddenly and sometimes rising to as much as Force 8 in the gusts. Meanwhile the barometer, after perhaps a small rise initially, will fall again. This is caused by low-pressure troughs which sometimes follow behind a cold front. There can be two possible consequences:

(i) the wind will eventually veer substantially along with a rising barometer to indicate that a definite weather improvement is on the way; meanwhile showers will remain, possibly heavy, with the possibility of thunder.

(ii) the barometer continues to fall as cloud cover increases, indicating the approach of yet another vigorous low.

The general appearance of the sky after a low has gone by, is often distinctive. The day, generally, seems brighter, the sea shows dark-blue wind ruffles, the sky is a clean, fresh blue clotted with fragments of cumulus.

Chapter Fourteen

QUICK-SILVER WARNINGS

For some reason or another there are only about a handful of barometric weather lores which, these days, are regularly quoted:

> *When the glass falls low,*
> *Prepare for a blow;*
> *When the glass rises high,*
> *Let the light duck fly.*

> *At sea with a low and falling glass,*
> *The green hand sleeps like a careless ass;*
> *But only when it is high and rising,*
> *Will slumber trouble a careful wise one.*

> *When rise begins after low,*
> *Squalls expect, and a clear blow.*

> *First rise after very low,*
> *Indicates a stronger blow.*

> *Long foretold, long past;*
> *Short warning, soon past.*

Reliability rating: excellent. The second one, in particular, may be a shocking rhyme, but they all provide excellent weather clues, probably the reason why they are so often hauled out and dusted by us weekend sailormen. It is odd though that there are a number of other equally pertinent and accurate sayings about the barometer's quick-silver ability to foretell weather changes which are not so well remembered.

129

A brief comment or two about the above barometer lores may be useful. By and large a falling glass indicates the probability of deteriorating weather, while one that is rising promises better conditions. There are provisos, though, and these are more or less covered by the rhymes; a barometer that rises steadily but slowly nearly always brings settled weather, but a rapid rise foretells the likelihood of some swishing squalls. Equally, as promised by the third and fourth rhymes, the first rise after a barometer has sunk to low during a depression is usually followed or accompanied by windy conditions. The final couplet carries with it a good deal of truth, too. The longer a barometer takes to rise or fall, the longer the weather it precedes will last; the faster the rise or fall, the quicker the approaching high or low will arrive, shed its cargo of weather, and bustle away.

It has become rather fashionable of late to decry the worth of the barometer altogether. In my opinion, those who maintain that the barometer at sea is not a very reliable guide are completely wrong. But then, so too are those who reckon a barometer often gives the only warning of bad weather a sailor will get. The barometer does supply a warning ahead of a real blow. It never, however, supplies the only warning; sky sign is just as apparent to seamen who have learnt to recognise trouble brewing in the wind. The weather glass is no more or no less than one of the tools at the disposal of the amateur meteorologist, but it should not be dispensed with.

Mind you, a good many of the barometers carried on little vessels these days are not worth much more than the ornamental space they take up. Often, they are so badly made that only the heaviest of forefinger jabs can stir them into life. Strictly speaking a barometer should never be tapped, although it is rare to come across any boat owner who is unable to resist a chance of flicking an absent-minded finger at the glass from time to time. The best of them can withstand a gentle tap, indeed, often need one. But the really inexpensive ones, which resist with sticky persistence the ups and down of barometric pressure, actually require a fairly meaty blow before unloosing their needles, leading to a couple of problems. First, because they are so cheaply made, they are nowhere near robust enough to put up with the constant heavy tapping. Secondly, because they only stir into life after a sharp reminder, it is easy to miss the rise and fall of barometric weather evidence.

So, get the very best barometer you can afford, and then get it properly set. Ideally it should have a range of 950 to 1050mb; more typically the range is less and about 960 to 1040mb. Many are set for something like 100ft (30m) above sea level, so before mounting the instrument, telephone your nearest Met Office and ask for the current value of sea-level pressure in your district. There is nearly always an adjusting screw on the back of the barometer with which to set the needle to the given figure. Once this is done, the instrument should faithfully register sea level atmospheric pressure.

Because it is mainly the rise and fall of the glass which is of prime concern to the weather watcher, a barograph is the ideal, although far more expensive, solution. This instrument, by means of a pen, continuously plots pressure changes onto a paper roll. If you can afford one, by all means do; if not, settle for the poor man's alternative and be content with plotting the barometer reading on a sheet of graph paper or in the log every hour, or at least on every change of watch. A warning, though; make sure that Tom, Dick or Harriet is not forever fiddling with the adjustable pointer which can quickly make it impossible for anyone to know exactly what the needle has been doing.

It is probably too old hat to even mention that the 'stormy', 'rain', 'very dry' sector markings provided by barometer makers should be totally ignored. Goodness only knows why manufacturers persist with them for they are, at best, no more than idiot guides to very little and, at worst, downright misleading.

It is useful to know approximately where the barometer needle ought to be according to the time of year. The average seasonal pressure in British waters is around the 1013mb mark during summer and about 1010mb during winter. A range of approximately 940mb to 1040mb takes the needle from an 'intense low' to a 'vigorous high'. There's one relevant saying I particularly like even though it may not be much in the way of a forecast.

> *The finest and most beneficial state of the atmosphere, more especially as regarding the health of man, is with a uniform pressure at a mean height of the climate varying from 29.80 inches to 30 inches.*

This remark was made by John Henry Belville in his *Manual of the Mercurial and Aneroid Barometers*, published in 1859. In the same work he commented:

> *During a series of stormy weather the mercury is in constant agitation, falling and rising twice or thrice in the space of twenty-four hours, the wind changing alternately from south to west and backing again to the south; this alternation of winds continues until the mercury rises to a bold elevation, when it ceases, and the weather becomes settled.*

That's a nicely worked observation on barometer activity during a depression.

On the whole, a reading around the 1016mb mark in summer indicates fairly settled weather. Once again, let me stress that it is the change of pressure, or its deviation from the norm, which is important, although a slight fall is by no means a warning to batten down the hatches and spread gloom and doom amongst the crew. In fact the glass may, and always should, fall for nothing more than the arrival of a shallow trough or a bit of low pressure which by itself presages nothing more than a cloudy day.

Normal daytime pressure variations, known as the diurnal range, also cause a slight but fairly regular rise and fall which is most noticeable (although only on the best barometers) during a spell of very settled weather. There is, in fact, a regular rise and fall twice a day – the greatest pressure generally being reached at 10am and 10pm. This, however, is hardly worth your while taking any notice of.

Generally speaking, any rise or fall between the 1000mb and 1020mb marks is an excellent pointer to a change in the weather, with the actual change depending on just how fast, how steeply, the needle climbs or falls. A steady barometer is one that changes by less than 0.1mb in 3 hours. One that is rising slowly changes by 1 to 1.5mb in 3 hours; a fast change moves 3.6 to 6.0mb in 3 hours; a rapid climb or fall takes place over more than 6.0mb in 3 hours.

As regards general weather guidelines indicated by this most accommodating of instruments, the famous generalisations laid down by Vice Admiral Fitzroy, who piloted Darwin's *Beagle* on its voyage of discovery in the nineteenth century, hold just as good today as they did 150 years ago:

Barometers rise for northerly winds including those from the north-west through north to north-east. They rise for dry or drier weather, for less wind or for several of these changes. The exception is when strong winds bring rain and snow from the north. Barometers fall for south winds (south-east through south to west), for wet or strengthening winds, or for a combination of these changes.

133

Reliability rating: very good. Successive generations of seamen have been able to observe the basic accuracy of these guiding rules and have refined them until today we are able to draw upon a wide range of barometric weather lores. It never fails to surprise me how many yachtsmen appear to have absolutely no idea what weather is on the way when the barometer provides such unfailing indications.

RISING BAROMETER

A rapid-rising barometer brings unsettled weather.

Reliability rating: excellent in general and certainly true whenever the barometer is 1018mb, rising rapidly, and accompanied by anything other than a southerly wind. A fast to rapidly rising barometer with a southerly wind, initially accompanied quite often by some whacking wind gusts, is generally followed after a short burst of rain by fine weather:

> *A rising barometer with a southerly wind, after some*
> *rain and squall, is usually followed by weather which*
> *in summer will be dry and warm.*

Reliability rating: very good. A rising barometer from anywhere between about 995mb and 1018mb is usually followed by moderate winds, probably from a northerly quarter, and rarely anything other than light rain. If the barometer begins to rise from somewhere below the 995mb mark, then:

> *When rise begins after low,*
> *Squalls expect and a clear blow*

Reliability rating: very good. Or

134

Fast rise after low,
Foretells a stronger blow.

Reliability rating: very good.

Air pressure which is rising, as opposed to that accompanying troughs and lows, may generally be regarded as a good-weather fairy. But the rule that any steep-rising high produces strong winds, especially around the outer edges of an approaching high-pressure system, should never be overlooked.

The most severe northerly winds occur after the barometer has shown the first signs of rise after very low . . . but good weather generally follows.

A rising barometer and falling thermometer means winds from the north.

Reliability rating: excellent for both. This is all part and parcel of the weather sequence experienced at the tail end of a depression. Once the barometer rises towards and above the summer average of 1013mb, the weather should improve dramatically; all northerly winds, with the exception of a north-easterly, blow themselves out fairly rapidly after the passing of a depression, leaving light to moderate winds.

When much rain falls with a steady rising barometer and the mercury attains a great elevation a long period of fine weather usually succeeds.

A slow-rising barometer brings settled weather.

A high-pressure barometer of 29 inches [982.5mb] to 30 inches [1016.5mb] and above that is rising steadily indicates improved weather.

Reliability rating: excellent for all three adages, which are as close to being immutable lores of the weather as it is possible to come. Almost invariably, when the wind is anywhere but north-easterly, a slowly rising barometer promises settled weather with clear skies, no rain and light to moderate winds. Given, however, a north-easter as part of the deal, rain is possible.

There are three typical barometer/sky/wind sequences which frequently occur when the glass is rising slowly. Mark them well for they, and their resulting weather, are to be welcomed when sailing on British waters.

1 *Barometer reading: slow-rising glass from below 985mb normally taking a matter of days.*
   Sky sign: big cumulus clouds with podgy cauliflower heads, good visibility.
   Wind: typically Force 3–4 NW or W.
   Trend: rain within an hour or so then dying out; wind high at first then decreasing, temperature cool.

2 *Barometer reading: rising slowly.*
   Sky sign: big cumulonimbus clouds turning to a greyish-black, almost total, cloud cover which appears to threaten rain but lacks the soft-greasy underbelly of typical rain-bearing clouds. (These hard, downward hanging blobs are what old folk call 'mamma clouds' because they look like the udders of a cow; they carry no rain or, at worst, only weak showers.)
   Wind: normally veering and increasing slightly.
   Trend: cloud cover will decrease, leaving a fine sky. The stratus cover above mamma formations indicates lack of viciousness in the wind. General weather situation will improve dramatically over the next hour or so while the barometer continues to rise. Only on rare occasions will anything more than very light showers occur; if they do, there is a chance that an old bad-weather front is being renewed.

3 *Barometer reading: rising slowly.*
   Sky sign: breaks appear in a gloomy-grey overcast sky as

136

a cold front passes away; fine-weather cumulus approaching from windward.

Wind: strong or fresh, slowly decreasing, often veering to NW.

Trend: cloud cover will gradually decrease – usually within 12 to 24 hours. Beware fast-rising glass and sudden fall in wind, which may well indicate a new depression approaching.

STEADY BAROMETER

There are times when a steady barometer is just as indicative of a new weather trend as a glass that is rising or falling. By and large, however, when the needle remains constant the weather will remain largely unchanged:

A steady glass, normal temperatures for the time of year and dry air means the weather will remain unchanged.

A steady low barometer is often associated with bad but settled weather; a steady high one with good.

If after a storm of wind and rain the mercury remains steady at a point to which it has fallen, serene weather may follow without a change of wind. But on the rising of the mercury, rain and a change of wind may be expected.

Sometimes fine weather occurs with a low barometer, but it is usually followed by a long period of wind or rain, or possibly both.

When fine weather accompanies a low barometer, a long spell of bad weather is promised.

Rain in some quantity may fall with a high pressure, provided the wind be in a northerly point.

Reliability rating: very good for all the above, each scoring a high accuracy mark of eight times out of ten during tests. There are a couple of typical steady-glass scenarios which also rate a high reliability rating:

1 *Barometer reading: steady after fall lasting several hours and then rising slightly.*
Sky sign: low stratus and stratocumulus begins to lift, traces of lighter sky breaks.
Wind: has been blowing fresh to strong with heavy gusts; now begins to veer.
Trend: rain, which has been heavy and prolonged, will moderate and turn to drizzle as cloud cover closes in again; wind will continue fresh with strong gusts behind lowest apparent cloud; expect substantial weather improvement in 12 to 15 hours.

2 *Barometer reading: high and steady, or rising slowly.*
Sky sign: no more than three-quarters of sky filled with cloud which is, ideally, mainly fair-weather cumulus; good visibility.
Wind: anything between light to fresh.
Trend: dry weather continuing with light to moderate winds by nightfall; sea breezes likely to develop during summer, spring and autumn when gradient wind is no stronger than light.

FALLING BAROMETER

Low pressure that is falling rapidly is a sign of the roughest sort of weather: strong winds, gloomy skies, heavy and prolonged rain – all the distinctive features of a low-pressure system.

Reliability rating: excellent. Old people used to say:

The lower the pressure and the stronger the fall then the more intense the storm.

It is an excellent rule of thumb.

A fall from 30 to 29 inches [1016.5–982mb] indicates a change to moderately bad weather, but when it begins to drop below 29 inches then look for something more than ordinary: regular slashing rains and gale-force winds.

Reliability rating: excellent, with tests proving that only the greatest and steepest barometric falls produce tempestuous winds and rains.

A steady barometer, a fair weather sky and a gentle breeze . . . a couple more sips of beer and I shall be away on the ebb tide

Falling pressure, after the barometer has been at its normal height for the time of year – accompanied by a rising temperature and increasing dampness in the air – foretells wind and rain from the south-west and south-east.

Reliability rating: good; in fact the adage would rate a much better marking if it had specified that the fall should be a steep and reasonably fast one, in which case future winds from a southerly quadrant are promised eight times out of ten. John Henry Belville (see also page 132), expanded on this theme:

If the mercury fall during a high wind from the south-west, south-south-west or west-south-west, an increasing storm is probable; if the fall be rapid the wind will be violent, if the fall be slow the wind will be less violent but of longer continuance.

The following sayings on weather conditions which track behind a falling glass have all been put to the test.

Pressure which is only sightly low [around 1000mb] and falling slowly, produces potential showers.

A rapid barometer fall with a westerly wind presages a strong blow from the north.

Any barometer fall of some depth after the weather has been settled threatens possible rain and wind squalls.

A falling barometer and rising thermometer denotes winds from the south.

When the barometer falls during northerly winds, look for storm conditions with rain, hail or snow.

A great depression of the mercury during frosty periods brings on a thaw. If the wind be south or south-east the thaw will continue. If the wind be south-west the frost will be likely to return with a rising barometer and northerly wind.

In the summer months, if a depression of two- or three-tenths of an inch [between 6.5 and 10mb] of the mercury occurs in a hot period, it is attended with rain and thunder and succeeded by a cool atmosphere.

Reliability rating: all better than 70 per cent.

Midday and the puddles are drying, for 'rain before seven, fine by eleven' is a fairly accurate observation of rain behaviour in the British Isles

141

Chapter Fifteen

COUNTRYSIDE LORES

Most of our weather lores originated either within the depths of Britain's countryside or upon the inshore waters which wash our coasts. There is one group of sayings which could have come from nowhere but rural Britain: those covering flora and fauna.

As weather portents they promise so much, yet most eventually prove a crushing disappointment. I still find it hard to believe that so many turned out such poor weather-tellers. After all grandfather and grandmother, and their great-grandparents before them, must have pinned touching faith upon the weather abilities of the birds and the bees, trees and the flowers; there are 439 or so ancient flora and fauna sayings which generations upon generations have turned into weather lore.

Collecting them together was difficult enough – picking up one from an old man in Shropshire, another from a little old lady in Essex and the odd jingle or two from an ancient, forgotten tome. Putting them to the test proved arduous, entailing endless hours peering at birds, weeks and weeks observing the flight of bees and bugs, and day upon day seeking wild plants in the fields and woods. I worked out once that I must have walked, cycled and occasionally motored, as much as 23,000 miles in first seeking weather sayings and then putting them to the test. At the end of it all I was left with only a fragment of the floral and faunal weather lores I started with, not much more than a handful which accurately predicted the weather they more or less promised.

It is no doubt instructive that the good Shepherd of Banbury (see page 56) in all his twenty-six rules for judging weather changes never once even hinted at bird behaviour or animal eccentricities. And you would think, would you not, that an Oxfordshire shepherd living in the days when there was still time to stand and stare would have given a passing thought or two to the birds of the air and the beasts of the field if there was anything special in their weather-telling abilities? So, when all is said and done, it should have come as no surprise that

If old sheep turn their backs towards the wind, and remain so for some time, wet and windy weather is coming,

proved a near total flop. The only time that I saw sheep with their backs obligingly and unmistakenly turned to the wind in all of eighty-one observations was when it was already blowing half a gale and the rain was ripping across pastures, sheep and me in sheets of rippled water. It was no less a disappointment that

When sheep do huddle by tree and bush,
Bad weather is coming with wind and slush,

scored no better than a pathetic 24 rights compared with 172 wrongs and proved, so far as I am concerned, nothing but quaint bilge.

There is a picture in the mind's eye of an old twerp with a desire to make rhymes, chuckling with glee all over his stubbled face when he first produced that couplet. No doubt he conveniently pronounced the word 'slush' as 'sloosh' so that it would rhyme neatly with 'bush'. Did he ever suspect that generations hence some equally stupid twerp would also be huddled by tree and bush in order that his saying could be put to the test, or wonder if his

143

'If fowls roll in the sand, rain is at hand' – a charming saying but all piffle and bilge!

children's children, and all those begat after that, would fall for this and other sayings? But we do. Countrymen all over the British Isles will quote, at the drop of a price of a pint, all sorts of nonsense weather rhymes and oblige with a knowing nod. The following are just a selection of some of the silliest. For all that, though, don't they have a lot of charm?

> *If fowls roll in the sand,*
> *Rain is at hand.*

This is just one of twenty-two sayings I managed to find which are to do with domestic fowl and the weather. Even Sir Francis Bacon had a stab at penning one:

Ducks prune their feathers before a wind, but geese seem
to call down the rain with their importunate cackling.

So, on the strength of this and others like it I haunted farmyards for nigh on four summers and three winters. My conclusion: any promise that fowls roll in the dust before it rains is, like any link with greese cackling and wet weather, purely coincidental.

I used to keep ducks once, before, one by one, they disappeared into the belly of a marauding fox. They used to preen their feathers whatever the weather past, present or future because that was the only way they could stay afloat – by working some of the body oils through their plumage. But then perhaps my ducks were not like others. I can believe it. As good, domesticated birds they couldn't fly; the books gave me their authoritative word that they couldn't. And so I used to tell my ducks, as they persistently stuttered skywards on stubs of khaki wings before swooping in a huge spiral towards the village shop where crimson-lipped children would drop ice-lolly fragments at their feet.

Any suggestion that geese cackle ahead of rain is just as daft as

> *The goose and the gander,*
>   *Begin to meander,*
> *The matter is plain,*
>   *They are dancing for rain.*

I used to keep geese as well, along with a small herd of goats, in a watermeadow near my home. While the ducks went on flutterbout, the geese and goats went on regular rambles without either my say-so or my blessing because they felt like it and not, my records of their walkabouts show, because they were carrying out some sort of primitive rain dance. If they were, it was only on something like a fifty-fifty basis.

There are any number of just as dotty bird sayings, for example,

If owls hoot at night expect fair weather.

Tell that to the owls! They mostly hoot because by doing so the tiny scampering morsels upon which they dine freeze in fright, and so become conveniently easy for owlish beaks to gobble down. Others are:

Pigeons wash before rain.

Balderdash!

If robins are seen near houses it is a sign of rain.

Piffle!

Sea-mews [a nice, old-fashioned name for seagulls] early in the morning make a gaggling more than ordinary when it will be a stormy and blustery day.

Poppycock! The strident gaggling of sea-mews, in fact, is heard loudest just after, not before, a storm, while they gather in squabbling gangs over bits and pieces of more or less inedible flotsam and jetsam.

The chirping of the sparowe in the morning signifyeth rayne.

Bilge! This is another daft adage; what a pity, though. How nice it would be, how convenient, if the met man imprisoned within the walls of Bracknell could pop outside from time to time and predict:

Hark! I hear the asses bray;
We shall have some rain today.

146

'Hark! I hear the asses bray; we shall have some rain today.' Poppycock!

Or how cosy if the TV meteorological expert could be televiewed before a roaring winter fire with a purring tabby upon his lap to pronounce:

> *If the cat washes her face o'er the ear,*
> *'Tis a sign that weather'll be fine and clear.*

It is puzzling that so many old country saws which have been handed down, through the centuries, prove so unreliable. The old farmhand, the hedger, the ditcher, the lad who chased crows, should all have known what they were talking about, surely. How come, then, that out of 155 countryside sayings about birds – all of which were optimistically put to the test – only eleven passed with marks better than six out of ten? Or that only two of the ninety-six saws about animals (including, purely for convenience sake, those relating to fish), proved anything more reliable than the toss of a coin. No matter; let the old adages forever be handed on by word of mouth. No matter that they make no practical sense. Long may they continue to be part and parcel of our heritage. Long may your children and mine, and their children – even when this green and pleasant land has disappeared into a tarmac weave of motorways – still repeat the foolish and the wise of our forefathers' weather sayings.

Meanwhile, I conclude with the following reliable floral and faunal tributes.

BIRDS

Take a tip from one who finds it hard to leave the sheets before the sun has risen. Just for once, break the habit; get up, be out and about near some hedgerow or coppice before daybreak and listen to the dawn chorus. If the day is to be a generally fine one, it will be like listening to the first stirrings of a newer, cleaner, fresher world; for the dawn of any day is worth singing about. In any case there's a six out of ten chance that the birds will forecast the day's weather for you. For

> *If birds begin their early morning chorus and then stop after some ten minutes, whether or not they resume again later, the day will be an unsettled one.*

> *If there is no dawn chorus, expect thunder.*

Reliability rating: fairly good, with both sayings scoring just better than 60 per cent accuracy. The first saying comes from Oxfordshire; the second, so far as I can make out, from all over England.

> *Doves or pigeons coming later home to the dovecote in the evening than ordinary, is a token of rain.*

> *If pigeons return home slowly, the weather will be wet.*

Reliability rating: just better than fifty-fifty; in fact test observations conducted on my behalf by two friends with pigeons in each case produced a 57 per cent chance of rain when the birds returned to their lofts much slower than expected.

This confirms my own haphazard observations of feral pigeons in residence in the castle ruins at Rochester, Kent: they are slower to roost when there is a change for the worse in the weather. They may know just what is approaching and are making the most of a dry spell during which they can cram their crops, before a period of enforced famine. On the other hand, a much more convincing reason is that advanced by scientists, namely that as pigeons apparently navigate by the sun, a lowering cloud layer makes any homing journey that much harder. And lowering cloud, as you know, often precedes rain.

When rooks seem to drop in their flight, as if pierced by shot, it is said to foreshadow rain.

The tumbling of rooks foretells rain.

If rooks twist and turn on leaving their nest, rough weather is approaching. If they stay by their nest, screaming raucously, gales are on the way.

Reliability rating: tentatively six and seven out of ten for the first two sayings; possibly similar for the third. Rook lore among country people is prolific, not only in terms of weather lore but in all sorts of other ways. They are, for instance, said to perch in circles before a criminal rook in order to pass judgement; and they supposedly maintain a 'rook parliament'. I hesitate to apply any reliability rating for the last saying above as I lack sufficient data. Privately, though, and based on only a handful of sightings, I temporarily award it a chance of proving correct six times out of ten – and I hope better of it. All rook sayings about their tumbling, twisting and diving displays foretelling weather deterioration are commended as reliable on a seven times out of ten basis.

'If rooks twist and turn on leaving their nest, rough weather is approaching' – seven out of ten for accuracy

I have no idea just why rooks prove such excellent prophets. Ornithologists, with whom I have spoken, were not able to offer any explanation either, although they all were convinced that rooks tumble 'as if pierced by shot' only before a definite deterioration in the weather takes place. They were equally sure than an especially noisy rookery indicates unsettled weather on the way.

Like rooks, plovers also appear to be weatherwise.

> *When plovers fly high and then low, making plaintive cries, expect fine weather.*

Reliability rating: 66 per cent, based on a total of forty-one sightings. Equally reliable is

Seagull, seagull, sit on the sand,
It's ne'r good weather when you're on the land.

Reliability rating: 77.8 per cent. A total of 221 logged sightings of unusually large gatherings of seagulls far inland was followed by poorer weather on exactly 172 occasions.

When larks fly high and sing long, expect fine weather.

Reliability rating: 76 per cent accuracy. Good weather remained for at least twelve hours after sighting high-flying, long-singing larks 93 times out of 122.

If swallows fly high the weather will be fine.

Reliability rating: most swallow sayings maintain that high flying predicts good weather (which tests prove that it does, 72 per cent of the time), while low soaring predicts rain. In fact it only rained on 47 per cent of the occasions when swallows were seen to be flying low. The saying is just as applicable to swifts and martins which fly high ahead of high-pressure weather.

BATS

If bats abound and are vivacious, fine weather may be
expected.

Reliability rating: 80 per cent. A similar adage is mentioned on page 95.

FISH

When the wind is in the east, then the
fishes bite the least;
When the wind is in the west, then the
fishes bite the best;

When the wind is in the north, then the
  fishes do come forth;
When the wind is in the south, it blows
  the bait in the fish's mouth.

Reliability rating: very doubtful. I have no real facts and figures to prove or disprove these adages. Seven freshwater anglers whom I questioned about the rhymes convinced me that at least some of the sayings contain more than a mite of truth. My own limited observations seem to indicate, though, that they rarely qualify as weather-forecasting omens. Fish don't, for instance, stop feeding before the coming of an easterly, but rather when the easterly has been around long enough to cool the water. On the same basis, a prolonged southerly warms the water and frequently turns the most timid of fishy species into veritable gluttons for tasty bait.

HONEY BEES

When bees to distance wing their flight,
  Days are warm and skies are bright;
But when their flight ends near their home,
  Stormy weather is sure to come.

Reliability rating: good. Bees fascinate me, so it was no hardship to spend a couple of summers watching the comings and goings from a neighbour's hives. Whenever the occupants lingered not much more than a stone's throw from the hive, there was a 73 per cent chance of rain falling within six hours. But whenever they constantly disappeared out of sight beyond the adjoining orchard fence, the weather remained good for twelve hours at least.

Mind you, there were always one or two mavericks who always did their own thing, so I learnt never to predict either rain or fine weather until a goodly number of the hive's residents buzzed off one way or the other.

'If the red pimpernel has its flowers fully open . . . there will be no rain that day' proved accurate for 92% of observations

PLANTS AND FLOWERS

Pimpernel, pimpernel, tell me true,
Whether the weather be fine or no.

Reliability rating: excellent, scoring an amazing 92 per cent accuracy during tests. No wonder, then, that the Scarlet Pimpernel is one of the most famous weather-tellers of the English countryside. Better known that the Wood Anemone which is said to

Close its petals before rain,

more often quoted as the 'ploughman's weather glass' than Chickweed which, one old adage promises,

Expands its leaves boldly when fine weather is to follow, but if it should shut the traveller is wise to put on his greatcoat.

The Scarlet Pimpernel has been given all manner of nicknames: Change of Weather, Grandfather's

153

Weatherglass, Old Man's Weatherglass, Poor Man's Weatherglass, Shepherd's Calendar, Shepherd's Dial, Weather Teller, and Weather Flower.

It deserves its place in the annals of English weather lore, for as another old saying has it:

> *If the red pimpernel has it flowers fully open first thing in the morning, no matter what the barometer may indicate, it will be a sign to say that there will be no rain that day.*

When the flower opened during the day-time dry weather occurred for at least six hours – and usually all day long – on 92 per cent of occasions.

Sadly, though, the standard-quoted corollary does not give the same excellent results:

> *If the petals are still closed first thing in the morning, rain is on its way.*

Reliability rating: poor. When the petals were closed, rain followed on only 17 per cent of observed occasions. So, count on the Scarlet Pimpernel as an excellent weather-prophet for fine weather, but a rotten forecaster for rain.

BIBLIOGRAPHY

The following list includes all the publications about the weather which I have found useful. Most are, unfortunately, now out of print but should be available from either second-hand bookshops or your local library.

Aristotle. *Meteorologica: with an English translation by H.P.D. Lee* (Heinemann, 1952). So far as we can make out *Meteorologica*, originally published in the fourth century, was the first book ever written about the weather. For the amateur weather forecaster it is of purely academic interest.

Booth, Derrick, *The Backpacker's Handbook* (Letts, 1979). This one contains only a single chapter on the weather, but it is so well written and reflects such sensible observation of sky signs that it is recommended.

Bowen, David. *Weatherlore for Gardeners* (Thorsons, 1978). A nice, basic guide for gardening enthusiasts which includes details on plant weatherlores and a few interesting comments on frost warnings – but treat many of the adages with suspicion.

Brain, J. P. 'Halo Phenomena – An Investigation', *Weather Magazine* (Volume 27, pages 409–10, 1972). Report on a quasi-scientific study of sun halos of only minor interest to amateur weather forecasters.

Claridge, John. *The Country Calendar, or The Shepherd of Banbury Rules to Judge the Changes of the Weather* (Sylvan Press, 1946). One of the first books entirely about weather lores was originally published in 1744 and written by John Claridge (shepherd) who almost certainly was the shepherd of Banbury, Oxfordshire. There are twenty-six rules containing nonsensical or accurate old saws by which, claimed the original manuscript, 'you may know the weather for several days to come, and in some case for months. . .'.

Constance, A. *The Inexplicable Sky* (Laurie, 1946). An attempt – not always a successful one – to explain weather portents contained in the sky.

Courtney, William. *What Does a Barometer Do?* (Muller, 1968). A children's guide to the barometer and, therefore, concise and easy to read.

Gates, Ernest Samuel. *The Amateur Weather Forecaster* (Harrap, 1965). Tends to drift off into realms of non-essentials about scientific meteorological principles and so forth, but nevertheless provides a useful description of amateur weather forecasting.

Gibson, C. E. *Be Your Own Weatherman* (Arco, 1963). A nicely practical, nuts-and-bolts book about weather forecasting for the outdoor enthusiast.

Inwards, Richard. *Weather lore: the unique bedside book taken from the world's literature and the age old wisdom of farmers, mariners, bird watchers* ... (Rider, 1950). Re-issue of an 1898 compilation of old weatherlores, 'concerning flowers, plants, trees, butterflies, birds, animals, fish, tides, clouds, rainbows, stars, mock suns, mock moons, haloes. . .'.

Meteorological Office. *Cloud Types for Observers* (HMSO, 1982).

Meteorological Office. *The Observer's Handbook* (HMSO, 1980).

Murchie, G. *Song of the Sky* (Secker & Warburg, 1955). Although, generally speaking, the title is the best part of this book, there are some fairly useful references to sky sign.

Rantzen, M. J. *Little Ship Meteorology* (Jenkins, 1961). Something of a curate's egg; quite good in parts, dull –

deadly dull – in others.

Roth, Gunter Dietmar. *Weather Lore for Sailors and Windsurfers* (E.P. Publishing, 1983). A basic book on mariner's weather lores.

Russell, Spencer C. 'A Red Sky and Night . . .' *Meteorological Magazine* (Volume 66, pages 15–17). Source reference for some of the 'red sky at night' principles mentioned in my text.

Silvester, Norman L. 'Notes on the Behaviour of Certain Plants in Relation to the Weather' *Quarterly Journal of The Royal Meteorological Society* (Volume 52, pages 15–23). Another source reference, this time on plant behaviour.

Unwin, David J. *Mountain Weather for Climbers* (Cordee, 1978). Contains some nicely observed facts on weather signs in the mountains.

Watts, Alan. *Wind and Sailing Boats* (David & Charles, 1973). Out of print, and, seemingly, difficult to obtain, which is a pity as this book contains some exceeding useful facts for sailing enthusiasts.

Watts, Alan. *Instant Weather Forecasting* (Adlard Coles, 1968). A 24-colour-photograph guide to weather forecasting using cloud and sky signs.

INDEX